JACK AND MR. GRIN

ANDERSEN PRUNTY

Jack and Mr. Grin
Grindhouse Press #104
ISBN: 978-1-957504-18-6
Copyright © 2008, 2024 by Andersen Prunty
www.notandersenprunty.com
Cover design copyright © 2024 by Andersen Prunty
Front cover image by fran_kie/Shutterstock.com
Back cover image by Lightspring/Shutterstock.com

Published by Grindhouse Press
POB 540
Yellow Springs, Ohio 45387
www.grindhousepress.com

JACK AND MR. GRIN

Also by Andersen Prunty

<u>Novels & Novellas</u>

Dreaditation
Neon Dies At Dawn
Irrationalia
Failure As a Way of Life
This Town Needs a Monster
Squirm With Me
Sociopaths In Love
The Warm Glow of Happy Homes
Satanic Summer
Fill the Grand Canyon and Live Forever
Fuckness
The Sorrow King
Morning is Dead
My Fake War
The Beard
Zerostrata
Jack and Mr. Grin

<u>Collections</u>

Bodies Wrapped in Plastic and Other Items of Interest
Deathtripping: Collected Horror Stories
Creep House: Horror Stories
Bury the Children in the Yard: Horror Stories
Pray You Die Alone: Horror Stories
Sunruined: Horror Stories
The Driver's Guide to Hitting Pedestrians
Hi I'm a Social Disease: Horror Stories
Slag Attack
The Overwhelming Urge

ONE

A perfect fall day. Jack reclined in the seat of his car, watching the fluffy white clouds drift across the deep blue sky, dreading going back into work. It was always during lunch the dread set in. That was when he had the desire to just fire up the ignition and drive home. But he needed the money. Needed the money just to live and, having no college education or any sort of trade skills, this was the job he was forced to take. At least it was nine to five so he could spend his evenings at home with Gina.

The windows of the car were rolled down and clean-smelling air filtered through it. He'd like to just lie outside all day on a day like this. Find a nice green meadow somewhere and just lie on his back and stare up at all the clouds and how they would change and come and go all day. He looked at the digital clock set in the car stereo. Only fifteen minutes left. Classical music floated and tinkled from the speakers. He didn't know the names or the composers of this music until the broadcaster told him but he liked the sound of it. It was relaxing, peaceful, beautiful.

He didn't have enough time to settle into a good nap so he moved the seat forward, looking at the wall of the building in front of him. There was a bit of lawn between the parking lot of his work and this building. A shirtless man in a long bandana did pushups in the grass. This man had been out there, doing the same thing, forty-five minutes ago when Jack had come out for his lunch break. He must be exhausted, Jack thought. But the man, heavily muscled and glistening with sweat, continued to pump away. Jack pinched the little roll that had developed on his middle section since he and Gina had settled into their comfortable domestic routine and the sex had stopped being a daily occurrence. Perhaps he could stand to do some exercise.

He dismissed the notion.

He was far too lazy for exercise.

Taking a deep breath, he got out of his car, leaving the windows down, and began the long walk back to The Tent.

TWO

He didn't know why but the red and white striped tent was at least a quarter of a mile away from the parking lot. He always had to start back to work ten minutes before his break was over just to make it in time. Maybe, at one point, they had planned on expanding but, as far as he knew, there wasn't a giant demand for dirt packing.

By the time he made it back to The Tent he was breathing heavily and had worked up a pretty good sweat. The building being a tent didn't do a lot to alleviate the heat. It was nearly impossible to install central air conditioning in a tent. He was just glad the steamy days of summer were over. They did bring in a few space heaters during the winter so that had always been tolerable. But those mean, humid days of summer . . . It made him glad for the change in season.

He walked through the open door of the tent along with a couple other coworkers. The foreman, John Briggs, stood by the opening, the lower half of his face covered in a dirty painter's mask, and glanced at his watch, mentally making sure no one could forge their timecards.

Again, Jack was filled with the urge to simply turn and walk out. There had to be better jobs than this. But he always managed to rationalize it until he stayed. The pay was better than average—more than he would get just starting out anywhere else. And the insurance, while inadequate, was not overly costly.

In the middle of The Tent stood a giant mound of dirt. A man in a yellow jumpsuit hosed down the dirt. That was Carl. The reason he wore the jumpsuit was not work-related. It must have been sweltering inside that plastic-type material. The dirt had to be hosed down because they had turned on fans due to the heat and, if not hosed down, it was like a dust storm.

He reached his workstation just as the afternoon horn sounded. He took a deep breath. A picture of Gina, covered in grime, was taped to the wall of his workstation. The rest of the area was filled with small plastic bags, boxes roughly the size of hardback books, and a trowel. The middle of his work area was filled with dirt. Dark, rich, fertile-looking soil in a mound up to his chest. He would spend the rest of the day transferring this mound of dirt into plastic bag-lined boxes.

He put on his painter's mask and got to work. If he didn't wear the mask he could feel the dirt running down the back of his nose. He would cough it up. It was bad enough to feel it all gummed up at the corners of his eyes when he woke up in the morning whether he showered or not.

After working away for about an hour, Briggs came by to dump some more dirt into his station.

Jack folded up the box he was working on and started another.

"I noticed some of your boxes feelin' pretty light," Briggs said.

"Yeah?" He didn't really give a fuck one way or the other as long as he got a paycheck at the end of the week.

"Yeah. See, the key is to give the dirt a little spritz." Briggs reached down and pulled a green squirt bottle filled with water and spritzed the dirt with it. "See there?"

"That's genius, sir. I don't know why I wasn't doing that."

"That ain't all though. Then you gotta pack it in there. Really pack it, you know?"

"I'll pack it as best I can, sir."

"I'll be checkin' back with you."

"I'm sure you'll find much improved results, sir."

"I'm sure I will."

Briggs strolled back amongst the other stations, leaving so many questions unanswered. It had been nearly three years and still Jack wondered why? Why the packing of dirt? Where did the dirt come from? Where did the dirt go? What made this dirt so special? It couldn't be used for gardening in such a small quantity. All of the boxes in his station were pre-labeled. He looked at the one he picked up. It was headed for some country called Grisnos. Where the fuck was Grisnos? He would try to remember to look it up on the Internet when he got home but he knew he would probably forget. He forgot nearly everything about this place the moment he left. Most days, he tried to forget he even had a job.

Three more hours, he thought, looking at the picture of Gina, wondering how she was getting along at the cafe. At least she worked with interesting people.

He looked at a beefy lady in the station across from his. She lowered her painter's mask and snorted the dirt, leaving a smear across her upper lip. If Mr. Briggs saw her do that, she'd be fired, Jack knew. She put her mask back into place and hiked up her lavender sweatpants until the seam lodged firmly between her gargantuan buttocks.

Three hours. Three fucking excruciating hours.

THREE

Their bellies full and their libidos emptied, Jack and Gina lay on the floor, a cool breeze blowing in through the open windows. Now that it was dark, the air was almost chilly. Jack brushed a strand of her black hair back from her forehead, curling it around her ear. He smelled the top of her head. He liked the smell of her sweat. It was like an exotic spice. Something he couldn't quite place. He thought about the surprise he had for her and hoped she would like it.

Earlier, he had brought dinner home and, after washing up to his elbows, they sat on the living room floor and ate. He had planned to take a shower after dinner but Gina had advanced on him before he had the chance. He hadn't minded in the least but still felt compelled to remind her that he was filthy.

"I like it," she had said, nipping the hollow of his throat with her full lips, licking some of the dirt away.

"We'll get the sheets all dirty."

"Who says we have to go to bed? We can stay out here and you can get *me* all dirty."

That was all the initiative he needed. It had been quick and ferocious and wonderful.

Now it was over and he felt even dirtier than before.

"I think I really need to take a shower." He stared at the ceiling.

"I might join you."

He took another deep breath of her scent. If they took a shower, it would be gone until the next time they did this.

"Stop huffing me," she said.

"Sorry."

They continued to lie there, both wanting to shower but wanting to be there in each other's arms even more. They had all night to shower. Today was Saturday and tomorrow would be their only day to sleep in. Jack would be glad when he didn't have to work six-day weeks anymore even though he didn't have any idea when that would be.

FOUR

Jack sipped his coffee and stared at the viney plant hanging from the ceiling. Green and growing nicely, its fist-sized leaves caught the early morning sunlight. It was Sunday. His favorite day of the week. No work and he and Gina were able to lounge around the house or go out to eat and shop or, really, whatever else they wanted to do.

Gina was on the floor, on her stomach, wearing a tight black t-shirt and black underwear, her lower legs raised and crossed at the ankles. She lay in front of an old childlike record player, listening to a 45 by the Mailboxes. Jack looked from the plant to her back, her ass, her legs. He loved everything about her. He didn't care if they never went anywhere. He was perfectly content right where he was, sitting in a recliner and staring at this girl in front of him.

But he was hungry.

His stomach grumbled.

He took a sip of coffee and put the cup down on the end table. Coffee didn't do anything to curb the hunger and, while he would much rather sit there and watch Gina manipulate the record player, he knew the refrigerator and kitchen were completely bare. Unless he wanted to eat coffee beans.

"You hungry?" he asked.

She turned her head and said over her shoulder, "A little . . . you?"

"Yeah. Think I'm gonna go get some breakfast. Want anything?"

"Yeah. The usual, I guess."

"All right. I'm gonna put on some clothes."

"'Kay."

He got up from the recliner, undoing the belt on his thin coffee brown robe he'd found at the thrift store a few months ago and headed into the bedroom. Stripping off the robe and his green flannel pajama bottoms, he pulled on a pair of well-worn jeans (also from the thrift store), deciding the white t-shirt he had on was fine.

Going back into the living room, he grabbed the keys from the same end table where his coffee cup rested and said, "Love you. I'll be back."

"Love you too," Gina said, flipping the 45 to the b-side.

Stepping out into the morning sunshine, he walked across the lawn to his cheap Japanese car parked on the curb. He glanced to his left. Mr. Moran stood stiffly, his forehead pressed against an oak tree in the middle of his yard. Jack waved to him but the man paid no attention, lost, as he was, to the bark of the mammoth tree.

Jack opened the passenger side door, sliding over the middle console and positioning himself behind the wheel. The driver's side door had been inoperable for quite a while. He made decent money at The Tent. He could probably even afford a better car but it seemed like they never had time to go look for one and he didn't really have any idea how long his job at The Tent was going to last. Best not to enter into any long-term financial arrangements.

The only decent thing about the car was the CD player that had, mercifully, gone unstolen since moving to Alton nearly a year ago. He cranked the ignition and Ben Folds blared from the speakers. He thought about changing the disc because he had heard it so many times but decided to let it play because it reminded him of when they had moved into this house on Stokesbury Lane. While they had painted before moving all their stuff in, they had an ancient boom box (it had to be one of the first to play CDs), and this was the only one it would play.

The car belching exhaust, he pulled away from the curb and headed toward downtown, to Granger's, home of the Granger Ranger Breakfast Sammich.

FIVE

"What'll it be, pardner?" the tinny voice came through the speaker.

"Can I get two Granger Ranger Breakfast Sammiches and two hashbrowns?" Jack said, feeling stupid. He hated saying 'sammich,' but they would totally fuck up your order if you called it anything else. At first, he had thought this was just some kind of urban legend. Trying it one day, he found out it was completely true and if you went inside or back through the drive-thru, they would pretend you were never there in the first place.

"I reckon you can, pardner," the voice said from the other end of the speaker. "Please pull yer hoss around."

Jesus, this place was so stupid. If their food wasn't so good he would never come here. But there weren't a lot of places to eat close to his house and even fewer had drive-thrus. He really hated to get out of the car. It was embarrassing, having to crawl over the passenger seat. It was like announcing to the world that he was uneducated scum, quite possibly doomed to the packing of dirt for the rest of his life. He considered himself lucky the driver's side window actually rolled down.

He sat in the line, hoping his car wouldn't die. There were three or four cars in front of him.

Hunger wasn't the real reason he had offered to get breakfast. His hunger pains probably wouldn't have really bothered him until early afternoon.

He had a secret in the glove compartment. It wasn't until now that he thought about how stupid it was keeping it in the glove compartment. Anyone could have come by and stolen it. But it was so small they would have probably missed it. Opening the glove compartment, he pulled out the ring. It was white gold, a single solitary diamond set in the middle. It wasn't anything fancy but it had cost him nearly two weeks of pay he'd had to sock away a little at a time so Gina didn't know he was planning anything.

He wanted his proposal to be a surprise.

He didn't want her to have to prepare to say 'yes.' He wanted to see the look in her eyes when he popped the question and he would know—just from that look— if she wanted to marry him or not.

It would be out of the blue, too.

This was the third year they were together. They had talked about it a lot the first year and then decided they shouldn't rush anything— it was just a piece of paper, right? And so they had agreed to wait two full years before bringing up the subject.

Gina had been nearly married once before. She had lived for five years with some guy named Tim Fox. Jack had seen pictures of him but he had never met the guy. It was Gina's theory that, by the end of the third year, if you still want to be with the other person, then maybe it had a chance of lasting. Tim Fox had proposed to her during their second year together and Gina had said yes because she was only twenty-one and didn't know any better. She had stayed with him for the next four years, she said, simply because they were engaged.

He supposed he could buy that but he couldn't help thinking there was something else there. Like maybe she really did care for the guy. But thinking about that made him mad. He couldn't exactly explain it. Maybe some things didn't need explaining. He just didn't like the thought of her being in love with someone else. Someone who had come *before* him. Jealousy, he guessed. Probably nothing more.

He pulled forward and slid the ring into his pocket.

Today was the day.

SIX

He was so focused on the ring in the front right pocket of his jeans he nearly forgot all about the bag of breakfast sitting in the passenger seat. He nearly sat in it as he went to slide over and get out of that side of the car.

His heart pounded.

He was almost certain she would say yes but what if she didn't? That would certainly put a damper on breakfast. Perhaps he should wait until after they ate. But he didn't think he could do that. He didn't think he would be able to eat until he knew her answer to his question. They hadn't really talked that much about it recently. He just had the feeling they both knew it was going to happen.

But what if she didn't want it to happen? What if she was perfectly happy with things the way they were? Would his proposal ruin it?

How could it? It wasn't like they were going to get married on the spot. It was basically just his way of saying she was the one he wanted to marry. The rest he would leave up to her. If she wanted to go to the courthouse tomorrow and do it, he would be there. If she wanted to wait five or ten or twenty years, he would wait for her.

The ring tucked safely in his pocket, breakfast in a splotchy white wax paper bag clutched in his left hand, he bumped the car door shut with his hip. Mr. Moran was still out in his front yard, staring at that tree. Only now, thankfully, he sat in a lawn chair.

Strange fucker, Jack thought, glancing over at him.

Oh God, Mr. Moran was actually *waving* him over. Briefly, Jack thought about ignoring him, pretending he didn't see him and just moving on into the house. But he had made eye contact with the old man. Now he couldn't really avoid him without the old man *knowing* he was avoiding him.

Jack seized up, walking quickly into the neighboring yard. Maybe if he just assumed this air of hurry then the old man, prone to unholy lengths of rambling, would realize he had something else on his mind and let him off easy.

"Hey there," Jack said.

Mr. Moran looked up from his lawn chair and said, "Morning there. I suppose you're 'bout ready for breakfast?" He nodded toward the bag in Jack's hand.

"Yeah."

"Well, I won't keep ya. Just wanted to say hi."

"Always good to say hi. We'll have to have you over for dinner one of these nights."

"That'd be good. You take care of that one. She's a beaut."

"Thanks. I plan on it."

Jack nodded, turning to walk away from Mr. Moran.

"You ever notice . . ." Mr. Moran said, stopping Jack in his tracks.

He considered pretending he didn't hear him this time but instead turned back around.

"What's that?"

"You ever notice how a tree is so huge?"

Jack had no idea where this one was going. It sounded like something a five-year-old would say.

"Anyway . . . a tree gets to be so huge and it just stays standin' upright like that for years and years but did you ever stop to think about what's keepin' that tree up?"

Jack took a deep breath. "Not really. I guess. No. I haven't really thought about that."

"The *roots*. That's what's keepin' the tree up. And did you ever wonder about them roots. There must be miles and miles of um spread out there, under the ground, growin' into the pipes, diggin' deeper into the earth to look for some water and, above all, keepin' the tree upright. If lightnin' strikes that sumbitch and he falls into my roof, it won't be the *roots'* problem, I'll tell you that right here and now. It's kinda like an iceberg . . ."

"Yep," Jack said, already backing away. He had to end this or, he knew, Mr. Moran could go on all day. He could start talking about a tree and it would inevitably end up with him relaying some childhood story Jack had heard nearly every time he spoke with the man. And Mr. Moran's message was always the same. People were better "back then." Life was better "back then." Now was horrible. Every day was a torment, so filled with injustice. Teenagers—hell, *kids*—were all assholes. His family didn't care about him. Nobody took any pride in their houses. The neighborhood looked like a shambles compared to a million years ago. Oh, Mr. Moran could go on and on and on. Jack had trouble with this single-minded, single-sided type of banter. Not to mention the repetition . . .

"I'm sorry, Mr. Moran," he said. "But breakfast is getting cold. You don't wanna get me yelled at, do ya?"

"They say the tip of the iceberg is only 'bout ten percent of the actual iceberg. The rest is underwater. That means, most of the iceberg, you don't even see."

By this time, Jack had backed across his neighbor's driveway and stood at the perimeter of his own yard. "Later, Mr. Moran," he said, raising the bag of food as if a visual reminder would help a little more.

"Yeah, yeah," the old man waved. "Call me Dick."

Jack turned and walked quickly, head down, up the porch steps, hoping Mr. Moran would not stop him again.

Call me Dick, he thought. Yeah. Well, probably not anytime soon.

His heartbeat picked up again.

Standing at the front door, he was surprised his conversation with the neighbor hadn't brought Gina outside to see what was taking him so long. She was usually pretty good at rescuing him from Mr. Moran. Maybe she didn't want to put on pants. Maybe she hadn't even heard them. Probably not, if she was still listening to that record.

He opened the simple white storm door, reaching his hand into his pocket and bringing out the ring. He palmed it and opened the front door, imagining Gina on the floor listening to her Mailboxes record.

She wasn't.

His heart continued to thud.

The needle of the record player had reached the orange paper label in the middle and made a horrible *screeing* sound as it whirled round and round.

The bathroom, he thought.

He walked across the living room and peeked down the hall toward the bathroom. The door was open.

Faster and faster his heart beat and he thought, this is it. This is really it. You're really doing this. Up until now, it could all be undone. But this was different. True, it wasn't marriage but it was something of a formal agreement. Things would be a little more set in stone after this.

Set in stone.

He didn't know how he felt about that phrase. It made him think of statues and tombstones.

Maybe she's putting on some clothes.

Now his heart was practically racing. It felt like it was bouncing back and forth between his nipple and his spine.

"Gina!" he called.

No answer.

Where could she be?

His heart reached maximum velocity as he began his search of the house. His heart was not going to slow down anytime soon.

SEVEN

Now his mind raced along with his heart. Thoughts swarmed around— crazy thoughts— and he had to try hard just to focus on a single one.

Where *was* she?

He had, in only a few minutes, managed to search every nook and cranny of the house where a human could foreseeably be. Closets (he didn't know why she would be hiding in a closet), the attic, the basement, every room. He had even opened the oven to check in there even though he didn't really think she would fit. Upon opening the door, however, horrible visions raced across his head—her body, dismembered and bent into impossible shapes. In the course of human history, he supposed, stranger things had happened. Of course, when one stopped to consider the scope of human history, there probably wasn't a single atrocity that could be ruled out.

Jesus fucking Christ, Gina, he thought. Where the hell are you?

This was bad. Jesus, this *could* be bad.

Realizing he still held the Granger Ranger's bag in his hand, he set it on the kitchen table and went to find his cell phone. That was what people did during emergencies, wasn't it? Make calls? Was this an emergency? He didn't really know. But the way his heart and head pounded along, it certainly *felt* like an emergency.

Deciding to go directly to the source of his worry, he called Gina's cell phone. She was number two on speed dial (voice mail was number one). He held down the button and listened to the phone ring, straining to hear if *her* phone rang somewhere in the house. It didn't. Which meant it had to be with her, wherever she was. Meaning she must have left. But he had no idea where she would have gone. They only had the one car. He used it to drive to work during the week. She worked at a cafe two blocks away and, if he didn't drop her off, she walked.

As the phone continued to ring, his fear mounted. She wouldn't have gone out for a stroll knowing he would return shortly with breakfast. Maybe she had been abducted. But who gets abducted before noon? And in their own home. Again, he supposed it could have happened but he just couldn't make this resonate in his increasingly cloudy mind. Abduction seemed so . . . cinematic.

Eventually, he was put through to her voicemail.

"Gina, this is Jack . . . I just came home with breakfast. Wondering where you are. Give me a call as soon as you get this . . . I love you."

Then he flipped his phone shut and wondered what to do next.

Mr. Moran. Maybe he was still outside. Since he had been out in his front yard when Jack went to get breakfast and he had been there when Jack came back, it only stood to reason he would have seen Gina leave the house.

He slid the phone into the front pocket of his jeans and went outside. He glanced over toward Mr. Moran's and noticed he was still out there. Now he circled around the tree, casting angry and suspicious glances at it. Jack wanted to check the backyard first. It was October, so it wasn't like there was any yard work to be done or anything, but it was an exceptionally nice day and it was entirely possible Gina had just wandered out there to take it in.

But why would she take her cell phone?

He felt helpless.

Mr. Moran's place was to the left. He took a sharp right, walking toward their driveway and around the side of the house. And then the back of the house. And then onto the other side of the house.

No sign of Gina.

He raised his hand to Mr. Moran. The old man said, "Short breakfast."

"Actually," Jack began. "We haven't eaten yet. I have maybe a strange question for you."

"Shoot."

"You haven't seen Gina, have you?"

"This mornin'?"

"Yeah."

"Nope."

"See . . . I'm a little confused. She was in there when I left and then, well, you know, I just came back and she's not in there. She's nowhere to be found."

"Maybe she stepped out."

"It's possible, I guess. But you would have seen her if she left, wouldn't you?"

"Well, my eyes ain't as good as they used to be. And I mostly been lookin' at this here tree."

"Regardless. I mean she's, you know, like human-size and everything. Kind of hard to miss, wouldn't you say? She would at least be like a big blur, right? Maybe even say hi or something?"

"I don't think I care much for your tone."

"Look, I'm sorry, Mr. Moran—"

"Call me Dick."

"Okay. Look, I'm sorry *Dick* but I'm a little . . . *frazzled* and just really really confused and I need all the help I can get so if you saw anything I really need to know."

"Nope. Sorry. Ain't seen nothin'. I'd let ya know if I seen anything."

"Okay. Of course. Yes, I know you would. So I guess I'm gonna go back in and make some more calls. Will you just let me know if you see her or hear from her? I know it sounds stupid. I'm probably just freaking out over nothing. But if you do . . ."

"I'll let you know."

"Thanks."

"She's so beautiful. I'd hate for anything to happen to her."

"Me too."

Jack turned back toward the house, already sliding the phone from his pocket. He didn't really know where he should call. He guessed he would try the cafe first. Maybe someone had called her, needing her to come in and work or maybe she had gone to pick up a paycheck or something but he knew she just got paid on Friday and he was almost certain she would have called him if she had to work. Still, he had faith in that reason. Yes, almost certainly, she was at work. People always called in on Sundays. Especially Sunday morning. People always called in hungover on Sunday mornings. That wasn't really out of the question at all.

He went into the house and sat down on the couch. He *made* himself sit down on the couch. If he didn't sit down, he was just going to nervously pace the entire house again.

Before he could punch in her work number, his phone rang.

EIGHT

"Jack Orange?"

"Yes." The voice didn't sound familiar. Or it sounded like any male who could have been calling. He felt like he didn't know anything anymore. "Who is this?"

"I just called to talk." The man sounded like he was smiling and something deep inside Jack knew that wasn't good at all.

"Who are you?"

"I think you know who I am."

Already he had a picture of this guy in his head. He was like a more bloated version of his high school history teacher. The teacher would come in and lecture for an hour about holocausts and smile the entire time. Only his history teacher had been very thin. Just from a couple of sentences, Jack pictured this guy as a plump man. He didn't know why. He was there, on the other end of the line, his plump red cheeks all pulled back, those white teeth, almost perfect enough to be dentures, gleaming out from all that rosiness.

And this man had Gina.

He either had Gina or he had done something with her.

"If I knew who you were then I suppose I wouldn't be standing here so confused right now," he said. His heart was really beating now. Already, his head raced with ideas of trying to track the man by this phone call. Of trying to pick up some sound from the other end that would allow him to place it. The sound of kids playing in a playground, or a siren from a fire engine, or a train. Anything. But he

20

didn't hear anything except for the man's somewhat labored breathing and, perhaps, the sound of his cheeks pulling back from his gums in that hideous grin.

"I wasn't talking about my name. I was thinking more generalized. You *know* who I am."

"You have Gina."

"That's right, Jack. I have Gina."

"But why?"

"Geez," the man said. "What would a man want with an attractive young lady? I could go into detail but I feel like that would be insulting your intelligence."

"You better not hurt her."

"Don't start with the threats. Not yet. I'm the wrong guy to be threatening, Jack. Besides, maybe you're too late. Maybe I've already hurt her."

"What do you want?"

"Do you honestly want to hear about what I want?"

"If it's money, whatever, just don't hurt her."

"But what if that's what I *want*? What if I want to hurt her? What if I want nothing more than to hurt her? Hurt her and do things with her?"

He resisted the urge to go off on the man. He couldn't afford to do that. Maybe if they were standing face to face . . . but they weren't. He was in the dark. Mr. Grin held all the cards. One card in particular.

"Besides," Mr. Grin said. "Don't offer me money. I know you don't have any of that. I know quite a bit about you."

"Again, what do you want? You wouldn't have called me if you didn't want something."

"Did you and Gina have fun last night?"

"What do you mean?"

"Fucking. Jesus, you're obtuse. Did you have fun fucking last night? That was the last time you did that, wasn't it?"

"How do you know that?"

"She has a nice little mark just below the neckline of her t-shirt. That's mighty big of you, to keep things like that away from the public eye. We wouldn't want her friends and coworkers or, God forbid, the *public* to think she was a nasty little slut."

Jack's heart continued to rage and anger surged up through him. At the very least, he thought, this man had removed Gina's shirt.

"But, you see, Jack, Gina *is* a nasty little slut. Bet you didn't know that . . ."

Jack desperately wanted to say something but he didn't think anything he could say would help his cause.

"Know how I know she's a nasty little whore?"

"How?" Jack spat.

"Because I've fucked her. I've fucked her quite a bit. And I want to keep on fucking her but you are threatening that. You're threatening to get in the way of all of it."

Now other thoughts were spiraling through his brain, none of them good, and he found himself inexplicably mad at Gina, even though he knew what this man said couldn't be true.

Or could it?

Immediately, he began thinking about the opportunities she may have had to cheat. Then he stopped himself. That wasn't really the issue now. That could only be a distraction. What he had to realize right now was that she was in danger and he needed to find her. He needed to help her.

"See, Jack, she's made it very clear to me that she would like to stop fucking me and keep right on fucking you."

"That's impossible." He couldn't help himself.

"Well, that's what I thought too. How could anyone want to stop fucking me . . ."

"You know what I meant."

"Oh, you mean it's impossible that she could be fucking someone else?"

"Yes."

"She's a very resourceful gal, that Gina. Anyway, I feel like you're not really listening to me anymore."

"I'm listening."

"Okay. So, in short, I don't want to stop fucking her. I like her pussy. I like the way she . . . shaves it."

A vice clamped Jack's heart, imagining Gina in some sicko's house, stripped down for his perusal and pawing.

"Now, I'm willing to take this like a man but I can't just bow out completely. What kind of man would bow out completely, without a fight?"

Jack found it very hard to breathe.

"Why, I'll tell you . . . it wouldn't be a man at all. It would be a pussy. I am not a pussy, Jack. *You* are a pussy."

This childish insult almost made Jack laugh out loud.

"So," Mr. Grin continued. "I've decided to give you a chance to find me. And I've decided to let you in on the rules."

"The rules?"

"Yes. The rules. Ready?" A brief pause. "If you go to the police with this, Gina is dead. Not just dead but tortured, degraded, humiliated . . . and then killed. And don't kid yourself by thinking I won't know if you go to the police. I will be the third person to know after yourself and the person who answers the phone at the station. So don't even think about that. Unless you like to hear Gina scream."

"Don't hurt her."

"You sound like a broken fucking record."

"What are the other rules?"

"That's really the only one. You have twenty-four hours to find me. That's the other one. After that, we will be so far away, you'll never be able to find us. You won't even know where to begin looking. Gina'd be plenty upset but, over time, I think she'd get used to it. And if you find me, one of us is going to have to die. So, therein lies your big ethical decision. Do you forget about her, convince yourself she's a lying slut and let us get on with our lives together? Or, once you find me, are you willing to kill another human to keep the one you supposedly love? Or, do you sacrifice her by calling the police and doing the 'right' thing?

"What'll it be, Jack?"

"I'm going to find you. And I'm going to kill you."

Mr. Grin laughed on the other end. "Well, then, I guess you'd better get busy, hadn't you?"

Then he was gone. Disconnected. And Jack stood there in the

living room, thinking how beautiful it had been that morning. But that now seemed like forever ago. This was not the same Jack who had stood there before. This Jack felt like he was actually mad enough to kill someone else. And that was something he had never felt in his adult life. He had also never even considered the fact of Gina's fidelity. He had trusted her with every ounce of his being. He didn't know if the call changed that. He desperately wanted to go out to the car and start driving, looking for her, but knew he had to put his thoughts in order first.

He took a deep breath and sat down on the recliner.

In twenty-four hours, he was either never going to see Gina again or someone was going to die. Both of those things burned him to his soul.

NINE

He had never been so confused in his life.

This whole scenario just seemed preposterous. Really, who did this happen to? He knew there were some people who found themselves, continuously and repeatedly, in odd situations. Trouble maybe. Some people were born trouble. It was like something in their brain just didn't function like other people. They always went about things the wrong way or did things they didn't really have any business doing in the first place.

Sitting in the recliner, he took a deep breath.

He was not one of those people. In his twenty-odd years on this planet, he had led a relatively trouble-free existence. He was born an only child and he didn't think there were that many kids who could complain about too much attention. No, he received just the right amount of attention. That was why his parents had only had one. Not for any physical reason and not because they wanted to dump all their attention and affection on this one single human. No. It was because they had their own lives when he was born and didn't plan on throwing both of their lives and interests away to focus on a slew of children. If they were strong individuals they felt he would be a strong individual. And he liked to think he was, for the most part.

He made it through school without being bullied. He could have easily gone to college if he wanted to but that seemed dull. He wanted to get out of the house. He wanted to be on his own. If he went to college that would be like tying himself to his parents for four more years, at least. Maybe this lack of trouble he had was more a sense of purposeless directionlessness.

Relationships were easily come by and just as easily buried in the dust. He didn't think of himself as an abnormally cold person but, realistically, he found himself with a girlfriend when he wanted something else to bury his cock in besides his hand and, eventually, he inevitably tired of this person because there was a lack of connection. None of them mentally turned him on. And he didn't think any of them could manage to physically turn him on day after day. Until he had met Gina. From the time he met her he knew there wouldn't be anyone else. If she didn't feel the same way about him in the long run and left him, he knew he wouldn't be able to stop her and he knew he wouldn't give up women but he *did* know she would be the girl who every further girl would be judged against. It wasn't any one thing he could put his finger on unless, maybe, it was mutual understanding. He knew what she wanted out of life. She knew what he wanted out of life. They made each other laugh. Life was better when they were together.

And even though they had lived, showered, and slept together all this time, he still found her mysterious. Occasionally, he would find himself wondering what she was thinking, knowing it probably wouldn't be what the average person was thinking. The way she moved, sometimes the way she talked, was completely different for him. He couldn't even exactly put his finger on it. It was like her smell. Something new and different and entirely her own and infinitely pleasing.

Now he found himself, absurdly, without her.

Was it possible she didn't feel the same way he did? If she didn't, it wasn't something she had ever mentioned. She had, many times, said things like, "When we get married . . ." or "When we have kids . . ." As though these were things they both knew were going to happen. And he had never intervened on those musings. Had never given her any reason to believe he wanted anything different.

Unless maybe he had just waited too long. That happened, he guessed. Women who wanted to get married waited for the boyfriend to propose and if he didn't do that in some mysterious allotted time only she knew about then maybe she grew cold and moved onto someone else.

But that just didn't seem possible. They had always been open with each other. About everything. Or so he thought. He guessed one person can never truly know someone else and maybe that was what this all boiled down to.

Now he had to think about finding her. Somehow this made him feel cheated. It made him feel singled out. Like God hated him or something even though he didn't really know if he even believed in God. This was an unrealistic challenge. One he felt like he shouldn't *have* to be going through. There were things he knew would come up. Jealousy over past loves. The threat of one of her coworkers, maybe. One who seemed to have much more in common with her. One who was able to spend more time with her. One who was a better match for her. Maybe they would develop different interests. Maybe she would get tired of him working too much overtime at The Tent.

He did not delude himself into thinking there wouldn't be arguments even though, thus far, that hadn't happened. Maybe they didn't know how to argue. Maybe that was the problem. Maybe she thought he hated arguing so much she couldn't truly open up to him, feeling like he would just say anything in order to avoid arguing.

He found himself the god of a whole world of maybes.

Maybe he should get off his ass and start looking for her. He could sit here in his chair and think his head off but that wasn't going to get him any closer to Gina.

God, this was just so fucking ridiculous.

He shouldn't have to be doing this.

It was really difficult to wrap his mind around something this insane. A needle in a haystack. And while he knew Gina, while he thought he would probably have definite ideas about where to find her, he knew nothing about her captor. Were they even in Alton? He didn't know, but he didn't think they could have made it too far. And were they even *on* the move? Would he be looking for a fixed location or would he be chasing them?

Okay. He had to think. He had to think about her and he had to keep the rules in mind, even though it was so fucking difficult to even take the rules seriously. This meant he couldn't really let anyone know she had been kidnapped because that person would undoubtedly go to the police. And he didn't have much time to work with so he had to act quickly.

First, he would go to her work. He didn't know what tack he would use but he would find some way to question her coworkers. Hopefully, Maria would be there. She was close to Gina's age and sometimes she and Gina went out and did stuff together. If she was having an affair, Maria would know. Then it would just be a matter of getting her to betray her friend and let Jack know who the bastard was.

He didn't really know what he could do after that. She wasn't exactly a social butterfly. She liked staying home just as much as he did. He guessed he could try her brother, Sam. He lived in Alton so he was relatively close. Her parents were out. He didn't want to worry them this early in the game. Maybe he could even try old Tim Fox. He thought he recalled her mentioning that he still lived somewhere around here. Hell, it was entirely possible Tim Fox was her captor. The man on the phone didn't really say he was *currently* fucking Gina. He had only said she had decided to stop fucking him and start fucking Jack. She had been in the decline of her relationship with Tim when he had met her.

More like stole her away, he thought.

Okay, yeah, maybe he had stolen her away but he didn't see how Tim Fox could be upset or bitter about that. From what Gina had said, he had a woman on the side too.

Whatever. It was time for him to go out and do something about it. If he lost Gina . . .

He didn't even know what would become of him. He didn't know what he would do. Spend the rest of his life looking for her, probably. So far, ever since meeting her, whenever he saw himself in the future, she had been a part of that future.

He opened the front door, ready to go, but things didn't look very good. Not good at all.

TEN

He stood at the storm door. The glass had been pulled up so the middle of it was just a screen. It would probably only be that way for a couple more weeks so they could suck in the last remaining smells of autumn before the wind became cold and they would finally have to shut the glass against the chill in a vain attempt to conserve electricity.

He smelled the rain even before he saw the black clouds plastered across the sky.

These clouds went beyond storm clouds. The last time he could recall seeing clouds like that was when he was sixteen, newly licensed, driving along the back roads of Glowers Hook, his hometown. He had looked into the rearview mirror and seen only blackness until lightning came and slit its fat belly. That was the first time he had opened up his car. He never understood reckless speeding before, never understood why that held so much appeal for kids his age. It seemed stupid, unthinking and uncaring. Needlessly placing yourself and others in danger for a momentary blast of adrenaline. But he had sped then. He was only a couple miles from his house, had never even driven in a rainstorm, and knew he did not want to be caught out in that.

Looking back at that storm, he remembered the strange things accompanying it. Reality mixed with town folklore, undoubtedly, but some things couldn't be denied.

People said all the animals left the Hook that day, running off to somewhere safe. Others said they saw no fewer than three tornadoes. Still others reported a strange purple glow over a section of the reserve and outlying areas. All of that could have been mere hearsay but the one thing that couldn't be denied was the ruination of the Turner property. One minute the house was standing and the next minute it had collapsed. Stranger still, no one noticed it for a few days, like something just caused the eye to glance right over it. And when they *did* finally notice it, they also noticed the mother and father were missing, along with a couple of other people from the town. The boy, Jack couldn't quite think of his name, was suspected, but nothing was ever proven because, try as they might, no one could find any motive whatsoever. It was written off to the storm.

An act of God.

God and his fucking acts, Jack thought. Yeah, he had had just about enough of God and his stupid fucking acts and tests— if that was what they were.

Standing there at the screen door, an overwhelming sense of awe swept down his spine. He couldn't let the storm hold him back, couldn't let it stop him.

When the first boom of thunder hit, he nearly jumped out of his shoes. His heart, which had been racing ever since he took the ring out of its secret hiding spot, now threatened to punch out of his chest. The thunder brought with it a sudden and harsh downpour of hail.

And it had been sunny only moments before.

He knew these were the worst storms. The ones that just blew up from nothing.

He would definitely have to let the storm pass before heading to his car. He had no intention whatsoever of getting out into that. It wouldn't be good for anyone if he was collapsed in the middle of the yard, bludgeoned by hail. He glanced over toward Moran's place and noticed the old man was *still* out there. Only now, the storm seemed to have taken his attention away from the tree. He held his arms out to the hail, his face raised to the heavens.

Jesus, Jack thought, that has to be pulverizing him.

He opened the screen door, forcing it against the wind.

"Mr. Moran!" he called.

But the old man was oblivious. He just stood there, holding his arms out as if to catch the hail, looking like a strange Jesus. He started moving around in a rapturous circle. Jack couldn't just stand there and watch him get blown to pieces by this storm. What if there was a tornado? What if lightning severed one of those branches from his beloved tree and it came down on his head?

Bracing himself, he grabbed a throw pillow from the couch, held it over his head, and stepped out into the storm. It was nearly as dark as night outside and it wasn't even noon yet.

"Mr. Moran!" he called again.

Walking quickly, he entered Moran's yard and put his free hand on the old man's arm. The saggy, paper thin skin was ice cold. The tree kept some of the hail away but he could still hear the pellets beating a strange tattoo on the pillow.

"Let's go inside, huh, Mr. Moran? Dick?" he said gently.

"No," the old man murmured.

"We have to. It's not safe out here."

"No." It seemed a struggle just for Moran to talk. Jack wondered if he'd had a stroke or something.

"Nowhere," Moran muttered. "Nowhere with you."

"No, it's okay. It's just Jack . . . Jack from next door?"

Now he tried to lead Moran toward his door.

"Goddamn you," Moran muttered.

"Come on, you'll thank me later." Jack thought that last part sounded lame but he couldn't think of anything else to say.

He walked Mr. Moran up the three concrete steps to his front door and pulled it open. Inside was dark. It smelled like burnt coffee and toast with a faint gaseous hint of that morning's scrambled eggs.

"Come on, let's just get you over to the couch."

"Get your *fucking* hands off me," Moran sneered this time.

Jack didn't know why his attitude had turned to such vehemence but he was now quite certain the man hadn't had a stroke. He tore himself away from Jack, turning around in his living room (the same size and shape as Jack and Gina's) to face him.

"You get the hell out of here."

"I was just trying to help."

"Call this help!?"

The old man stuck out his flappy, wrinkled left arm and pointed to a mark there.

"That ain't no help at all," he nearly cried.

Jack couldn't get close enough to him to tell what the mark was. It looked like a fresh tattoo, the way it was all puckered and red around the edges. Maybe even a branding. It was a rectangle, the short sides on the wrist and elbow ends, at the direct center of the inside of his forearm. There was another line through the middle of the rectangle so that it was divided into two squares.

"I don't understand what you mean," Jack said.

"The fuck you don't!" Moran snorted. "Ain't no coincidence. Your pussy goes missin' and then I get this."

Now Jack was really confused.

"I'm afraid I don't understand. Do you need me to call an ambulance for you? Do you need me to take you someplace? Are you hurting? Are you okay?" At this point, he was just throwing things out. He didn't really know what he was saying.

"I just want you to get the fuck away."

"Who did that to you?"

"Wouldn't you like to know?"

"Yes. You're right. I would like to know. It could be really important to me right now. Did someone hurt you?"

"God hurt me. God hurt me cuzza you."

"I'm afraid I don't understand."

"Lettin' you two live over there in sin. I didn't do right by God by lettin' that go on. I should uh been over there ev'ry day, lettin' you know the wages of that sin. Now I'm the one who pays."

Why did everyone's accent get worse when they were either drunk or talking about God?

"That's . . . *crazy*, Dick."

"Get the fuck outta my house. You ain't got no right to stand there and call me crazy."

"I just want to know who did that to you."

Mr. Moran grabbed a heavy plaster candlestick from the top of his floor-model television and held it up in his right arm. Jack couldn't stop staring at the mark on his left.

"Get the fuck out," Moran spoke lowly, slowly, murderously.

"*Who?*" Jack said.

Moran let loose with the candleholder and it drilled Jack in the right shoulder, despite his attempt to fend it off with the pillow, and then the man lunged at him. Jack didn't think now was the time to probe him any further. Now was also not the time to beat up an old man, candleholder throwing or not. Moran was not very fast. Jack hurled the pillow at him and jerked to his right, plowing through the screen door and nearly unhinging it.

Moran stood in the doorway and shouted at him.

"You'll see! This is your mark, Jack! Your mark! You'll see!"

The hail had stopped but the rain was still pissing and Jack planned on going straight for his car. He just wanted to be away from here. Halfway across his lawn, he seized up.

A large limb, hell, half the shitty silver maple tree in front of his house, had split and crushed the top of his car.

Standing there in the rain, the lightning dancing in the heavens above, he slapped his soaked thigh and said, "Fuck me."

Behind him, Mr. Moran slammed his door, opened his door, slammed his door, and opened his door only to slam it again.

Jack was very worried and very scared.

He turned in the direction of the cafe.

ELEVEN

He had to fight the urge to run to the cafe. Suddenly, it felt like his whole life had been thrust into some kind of terrifying fast-forward. But if his body went as fast as his mind wanted it to go, he would be dead by afternoon. He was slothful by nature. If it wasn't for his current predicament he would probably be sprawled out in the recliner, enjoying a nice little nap. That was what his Sundays were for. Laze. There were some Sundays he and Gina only left the bed to eat and use the bathroom. Those were beautiful, glorious days. If the whole world had more of those days, there would be a lot less hate. A lot less destruction. Forget about war. Stay home and fuck.

He walked quickly, taking measured breaths.

His phone rang, chiming from the left pocket of his jeans. Quickly, he pulled it out, noting the call came from an unknown number, and snapped it open.

"Yeah," he said.

"Some men are born to shake the walls of temples. Other men are meant to crawl through shit. Some men aren't men at all."

He recognized that voice. Imagined those jowls pulled back tight.

"Where are you?"

"I am the one who shakes the walls of the temple. You are a shit crawler. Or maybe you're not a man at all. Listen to this . . ."

He heard a scream pierce through his phone. Loud enough to cause him to hold it away from his ear.

"You fucking bastard."

"Careful, shit crawler," Mr. Grin said. "I think your little bitch has a lot more screams left. Bye now."

And then he was gone, leaving Jack with the emptiness Gina's scream caused. What could he have possibly done to make her scream like that? Visions of burning cigarettes on perfect pale skin screamed through his head. Other things . . . Fingernails pulled out. Nipples clamped. Arches jabbed.

He tried to shake them away.

Those visions were not helping. Those visions couldn't help him. They could only cause the hate to rise a little closer to the surface, clouding the mystery, muddling the game.

Grimacing at the brutal day spreading out before him, the brutal morning already buried in the past, shivering in his thin, soaked t-shirt and soaked jeans, sagging low around his hips, he trudged onto Corner Street, bringing the cafe into view. The rain continued to pour down, adding to the overall grayness now cloaking the neighborhood. His breath plumed out of his mouth and he found himself craving a cigarette, really *craving* one, for the first time in three years.

Very few cars were on the road. Obviously, no one was out playing in their yard. He felt like the most alone person on the planet. Except he wasn't. He knew, somewhere, Gina felt much more alone than he did. If he could only find her. That was all he had to do. Every second, his anger toward Mr. Grin doubled and trebled and he thought, by the time he actually found him, he would probably be able to tear him apart with his bare hands.

He nearly skipped across the parking lot to the cafe, eager for the warmth and its connection to people. People who were not crazy. People who didn't slam doors.

He pulled open the steamed-over glass door, immediately melting with the comforting scent of strong dark coffee. Maria was behind the counter, making some sort of frothy drink for a middle-aged woman. She noticed Jack. He noticed the curious look that crossed her eyes, probably wondering why he had chosen to walk here now, of all times, before she raised her head in a slight greeting.

He watched her go about her business, standing quietly and rubbing his bare arms for warmth. Maria took art classes at the community college. One of her parents was Filipino, Jack couldn't remember which one, and her thick black hair hung down to the middle of her back in perfect dreadlocks. This, of course, meant she had gone to great lengths in order to *give* herself dreads. Both ears were more gleaming white metal than flesh and other small hoops adorned her left eyebrow, her right nostril and the left side of her lower lip. Never minding how clichéd it all was, it managed to work on her.

She sat the cup in front of the woman. The woman asked for whipped cream. Maria rolled her eyes, pulled the aerosol can out of the refrigerator and sprayed some on top of the beverage, giving the woman a completely sarcastic grin. Jack noticed the woman's face as she turned away with her drink and thought she looked scared. Probably hoping her daughter never grew up to look like Maria.

"What's up?" Maria asked.

"Are you the only one here?" he asked, suddenly aware of how crazy and paranoid that sounded.

"No, Joey's in back. Why?"

"Do you think you could talk to me for a few minutes?"

"Sure. Are you okay? Is it about Gina? Is *Gina* okay?"

"I just want to talk."

"Sure. Hang on." She turned around and took a couple steps until she was in between the back counters, cracking the door leading to the back room and saying, "Hey, Joey, can you watch the counter for a bit?"

Jack heard a distant "Yeah" come from the back room.

Maria motioned for him to come behind the counter with her. He followed her into the back room, passing Joey on his way to the front.

"Hey Joey," Jack said.

"Hey Jack. Everything okay?"

"I think so." He sincerely wished he could offer something a little less ambiguous than that.

Maria held up at the last minute. "You want a cup of coffee or something?" she asked. "You look cold."

"Yeah. That'd be nice. Thanks."

"Be right back."

The back room consisted of a small burnt orange couch and an old Formica and chrome kitchen table with four black vinyl seats surrounding it. The tabletop was covered with magazines— *Rolling Stone*, *Mental Floss*, *The Modern Drunkard*, *Rue Morgue*, *Bust Down the Door and Eat All the Chickens*, and *Reader's Digest*. He thought that last one seemed a little out of character but who was he to judge? He pulled one of the chairs out and then decided he probably shouldn't sit down in it. He was still dripping. The heat of the cafe was nice. It made his skin sting and itch.

Maria came back with an ivory ceramic mug. "Black?" she asked.

"Yeah. Black is good."

"Sit down."

"I'm soaked."

"I don't think anyone's going to care. That chair probably cost less than a cup of coffee."

"Thanks."

He sat down at the table and took a sip of the coffee. It was hot and good.

"So what's up? I don't think I've ever seen you not in the same room as Gina. Is she okay?"

"Yeah. I think so. I just wanted to ask you if you've noticed anything odd about her lately."

"Odd?" Maria's silver eyebrow hoop rose slightly. "Gina's always been a little odd. Is she sick or something?"

"No. Well, I guess what I wanted to know was . . . do you think she could be having an affair?"

"An affair? Gina?"

"Yeah."

"Why?"

He noticed she asked why instead of flatly stating it was impossible. "I just . . . I don't know. I've been getting these strange phone calls and . . ." He realized he didn't have much to suggest Gina having an affair that wouldn't also let Maria know what was happening. And, of course, she couldn't know what was happening because that would go against the rules and if she decided to go to the police as any sane and rational person would then it was likely Gina would end up dead. He was not a good liar. He never lied. But he had to now. "Well, she said she was going out with some friends last night and she didn't come home."

Maria's jaw dropped.

"And I didn't know if you were with her or not. I know you guys go out sometimes. I was just wondering if she, you know, ever went home with any guys or, hell, I don't even really know what I'm trying to prove . . ."

"Usually, when we go out, she's the *driver*. I mean, I've been pretty wasted a few of those times and I guess anything would have been possible, I wouldn't have even noticed but, Jack, I think she's crazy about *you*."

"So, you never noticed anything?"

"I can say in good faith that I haven't. Do you know who she went out with?"

"Oh, it was her sister and some of her sister's friends. I don't know any of their numbers or anything like that or I'd try bothering *them*."

"Have you tried calling Gina's phone?"

"Yeah, but she won't pick up. I think she thinks I'd be mad at her."

"You want me to try?"

He hadn't even thought of that.

"Yeah. She wouldn't have any reason not to answer a call from you."

She walked to the back of the small room, to a coat rack, and reached into her dangling olive drab backpack, pulling out her phone. She opened it and pressed a button.

"It's ringing," she said, looking at him. Then a disappointed look crossed her face and she mouthed, "Voicemail," before saying into the phone, "Hey, Gina baby, it's Maria. I'm at work but call me when you get this, okay? Leave a message if I don't answer. Later."

"No luck, huh?" He knocked back another heavenly warm slug of the coffee.

"Nope."

"Damn."

"Are you sure there isn't something else going on? You guys get in a fight or something?"

"No. We never fight."

"I know. Believe me, I've heard all about the perfect relationship of Gina and Jack."

"Sorry," he shrugged.

"No. It's nothing to be sorry about. I'd take it if I could get it."

Maria reached a heavily ringed hand out and put it over his. "You should let me know if things don't work out between you."

His heart skipped a beat. My God, was she *hitting* on him? It put into perspective how not-serious his predicament seemed to anyone who didn't have all the information.

He took another shaky sip of his coffee and said, "Thanks for the help, Maria."

"Any time," she smiled.

He stood and paused at the door leading out into the cafe, turned, and said, "When you guys went out . . . was it normally just you and her or did anyone else ever go along?"

"No. It was normally just us. Sometimes we would run into people she went to high school with and hang around with them but never outside of the bar or anything."

"Like who?"

"Oh, just people . . ."

"Like ex-boyfriends and things?"

"Oh, you mean like Tim Fox?"

"Exactly."

"Yeah, we ran into him a couple of times but she never went anywhere with him. I mean, there was nothing there. Besides, he's married and has a kid and everything. You shouldn't worry about him."

Yeah, he thought. And Gina probably thought she didn't have to worry about you, either.

"No. Okay. Thanks, Maria."

He walked through the cafe and out into the cold noon drizzle.

TWELVE

Once outside, he stopped, turned, and went immediately back into the cafe.

"Hey Joey," he said. "You guys have a phone book here?"

"White or yellow pages?"

"White, I guess."

Joey reached under the counter and brought the book up, plopping it onto the counter, the smell of cheap newsprint wafting up from it. The front of it had an overhead picture of Alton on it. The picture was from far away—the further you got from Alton, the better it looked. Opening it, he flipped to the "F" section. If he was going to try and find Tim Fox, he supposed he should know where he was looking. A Timothy L. Fox was listed at 118 Ettinger Lane. He would just have to assume this was his man.

Or Gina's man . . .

He closed up the book and said thanks before a sound came from the back of the cafe, startling him. It was a very succinct scream. Almost more of a bark. Probably Maria, he figured. Joey's eyes grew wide and he started for the back. Jack held up a hand.

"Stay out here," he said. "I'll check and see if she's okay."

In the few seconds it took him to cross around the counter and get into the back room he had already hoped her scream came from something simple like pinching a finger or slipping or any other mundane household accident but, in the back of his brain, he already had thoughts that it was something more sinister. He couldn't help but think everything happening to him had something to do with Gina's disappearance—from the storm to Moran's behavior to his bizarre actions and now to something as minor as Maria's brief yelp.

When he reached the back room, he saw her standing in the middle of the room, holding her left wrist with her right . . . looking at her forearm. He thought he knew what she was looking at before asking, "Can I see?"

Her eyes were huge, her eyebrow ring now nearly meeting her hairline.

"What the fuck?" she said.

"When did this happen?"

"Just now."

"You're kidding." He thought her shout had been one of surprise more than pain given the rest of her prickly accoutrements and many other tattoos and piercings that were probably not visible.

"No. I was getting ready to come back up front and I felt this stabbing pain like something was biting me and I pulled up my sleeve and there it was."

It was exactly like the one on Moran's arm. A vertical rectangle with a horizontal line bisecting it, turning it into two squares. And it definitely looked more like a branding than a tattoo. He couldn't see any ink. Just angry red welts. Five altogether.

"What the fuck is it?" she asked.

"I don't know. How *could* I know?"

"I don't know," she mumbled, continuing to look at her new brand. "I just thought maybe you would."

"I haven't a fucking clue."

He could tell by looking at her she wasn't telling him something. Some people made good liars. Some people wore their lies on the crease of their brows and the depth of their eyes. Maria was one of the latter.

"What is it?" he asked, putting a hand on her shoulder, feeling the heat coming through the thin cotton of her shirt.

"When it happened . . . I had a . . . *vision* of you. Like I saw your face very clearly in my head." She bit her lower lip. "That's happened before but this was . . . different. Like I immediately associated the pain with your face."

"Interesting," he said.

"*Interesting?* I want to know what the fuck it is."

"It's probably been there all morning and you just now noticed it. It'll probably clear up. I wouldn't worry about going to go see a doctor until tomorrow. See if it isn't better."

"I don't like doctors."

"Who does?"

"Now what aren't *you* telling *me?*" she asked.

He couldn't help but laugh. "What am *I* not telling *you,*" he said. "Oh, there's a whole lot of shit I'm not telling you. I'm sorry. I really am but I can't. Really, it would probably be best if you just forgot I came here today. Will you do that? Then maybe you, me, and Gina can sit around in a couple of days and laugh about all this over some beers."

"Okay. I just want to make sure no one's in trouble. You kind of act like somebody who's in a lot of trouble."

"I might be," he said. "Just . . . you know, don't tell anyone what I asked about Gina. I don't want it to get back to her if she's not seeing anyone else. I don't want to look like a jealous paranoid ass-hole. And if she is, it'll really just be embarrassing . . ."

"I understand."

"You should come by the house tomorrow. If you don't hear from me or Gina before then, you should stop by tomorrow, maybe on your lunch break or something."

"Jack, what the fuck's the matter?"

"I can't, Maria. I wish I could. Boy, I really wish I could tell you. I think I need to go. Take care. Call me on my phone if anything else . . . *strange* happens, okay?"

"I don't have your number."

He went over to the table, grabbed the *Rolling Stone* and a pen and scrawled his number across Bono's forehead.

"There. Now you have it. Call me later."

"Sure," she said.

He thought about how important that later phone call might be. Once he knew where Gina was, he didn't care what Mr. Grin said, he would tell anyone he knew because he might just need their help. He might need all the help he could get.

For the second time in ten minutes, he left the cafe.

THIRTEEN

He felt lost. Alton was not an enormous city or a small town. It was a mid-sized city. Nowhere near as large as Columbus or Cincinnati. He thought he knew where Ettinger was. He didn't want to take any chances. A map was what he needed. And transportation. Transportation would have been a godsend. Well, he thought, there's always the bus. He had never ridden the bus but he knew it was available if he needed it. He always noticed bus stops but figured, now that he needed it, there wouldn't be one for miles. With his luck, he wouldn't be surprised if all the bus drivers had gone on strike.

Luckily, the rain had tapered off a bit. It was now more like a cool mist. This was probably going to give him a fairly horrendous cold.

But what would a cold matter if he didn't live another day? What would a cold matter if he lost Gina forever? Not one bit was the only answer he could come up with.

He walked to the edge of the cafe parking lot and looked around. The cafe was in a strip mall with a lot of shops that were essentially useless to him. But there, across the street, was a gas station. Gas stations, especially the ones with brightly lighted convenience stores attached to them, were the answer to most of modern man's needs and questions. Bathrooms, maps, food, coffee, cigarettes, gas—they had everything.

He headed in that direction. Gleefully, he noticed the tinted-glass awning of a bus stop in front of the gas station's parking lot. If he was really lucky, the clerk would know what time the next bus ran.

He gave himself fifteen minutes. If the bus was supposed to come within fifteen minutes, he would wait for it. If not, he would carry on. He pulled his cell phone out of his pocket and looked at the display on the front of it.

12:45.

It was hard to believe that less than two hours had passed since his horrifying telephone call. Consequently, that meant less than twenty-two hours remained for him to find Gina. And he still didn't really know where to begin looking.

He walked into the gas station. The clerk, a dumpy lady in her forties, nodded her peroxided head. He raised his hand and approached her.

"Maps?" he asked.

"Right under you," she said. Her name badge said 'Donna.' She had three blue stars below her name. He guessed that was good. Surely this woman with three blue stars would be able to help him.

"Thanks," he said.

He found one that would help him. It was a thin fold-out type for Alton and surrounding areas. Most of the surrounding areas were cornfields.

He put the map on the counter.

"That it?" Donna asked.

"I think so."

She gave him the total and he reached for his wallet. He didn't have any cash. He hardly ever carried cash anymore. Just some coins that hadn't fallen out into the washer yet. He gave Donna his credit card.

Damn. Lack of cash might be a problem if he was going to ride the bus. Last he'd heard, buses did not take credit cards. Although, to his knowledge, they might be the last places on earth not to do so. He would have to hope he had more coins.

"What time does the bus run?"

"Oh . . ." Donna seemed surprised. She handed his card back and pushed a piece of paper toward him to sign. "I think it runs about every half hour or so." She laughed. "Can't say for sure. Ain't never rode it."

"So . . . it'll probably be back around one or so?"

She craned around and looked at the clock behind her.

"I reckon," she said.

"Thanks."

"No problem."

"Oh, you don't happen to have an ATM, do you?"

"We do but it ain't got no money in it." She gestured to the useless machine in the back. "Never has no money in it."

He imagined her thinking money magically appeared in the machine.

"Well, have a nice day," he said, trying not to let his frustration show through a friendly smile.

He took the map and left the store. The paper turned immediately soggy upon stepping outside. He made his way over to the bus stop, grateful to be in the little plexiglass vestibule. He was the only person in it. He sat down and spread the map out before him. It had a street index, which helped a lot. Ettinger wasn't that far away at all. It was at the far side of his neighborhood, toward downtown Alton. He had been a street over when he went to Granger Ranger's that morning.

He looked at the map, studying the complexity of it. Gina and Mr. Grin could be anywhere, he thought. If they were still in Alton at all.

Some part of him still kept expecting to wake up.

He decided to spend his time waiting for the bus studying the map. Familiarize himself with the city. Basically, since moving in with Gina, he had driven to The Tent and back. That was it. When he was a teenager, exploring the roads, it had been in the small farm town of Glowers Hook. Those were the roads he "knew like the back of his hand." Alton's roads, well, maybe he knew those like the back of his foot or some other part of his body that spent most of its time covered up.

The layout was pretty simple.

From the city's center, a grid of streets ran north to south and east to west with clever names like First Street and Second Street. Not quite as large as New York, Alton's only went to Fifth Street.

To the east of downtown was the industrial sprawl that made Alton prosper. Steel mills, paper mills, rubber factories. And the slums. The little houses that were no bigger than trailers. And trailers . . . there were plenty of those, as well. He and Gina had lived in one for a year before finding their current home. To the south were the more affluent suburbs. These had names like The Oaks, The Woodlands, Alton Heights. To the north, roughly where he now sat, were the perfectly middle-class suburbs that took up most of Alton's geography. To the west there were very few roads. He figured most of that area was woods and fields.

He never really had much of a reason to go to that section of Alton, although he *had* been there before. With Gina, of course. He remembered a huge meadow and some train tracks. The train tracks were curious. There were two abandoned engines on the tracks and it looked like they had collided. The fronts of both engines were sort of rumpled and he had found this amazing. One of the engines still had a boxcar attached to it. This was where Gina had taken him. They had spread a blanket out in the boxcar and made love in a late summer sunset.

If they made it through this, he thought, he would take Gina back there and propose to her.

Screeching brakes snapped his memory back to the immediate present. He quickly and imperfectly folded the map back up and walked up the rubberized steps of the bus. He didn't have any idea how much it cost to ride. He dug in his pocket, thankful for the handful of change there. Without counting it, he dumped it into the machine by the hirsute, heavily tattooed driver and something dinged. Apparently he had met the minimum.

"I don't give change," the bus driver said.

"I know," Jack said. "Does this go by Ettinger at all?"

"Fifth stop," the driver said. He pulled his hat down low over his brow and pulled the pneumatic lever that sent the doors hissing shut.

There were five other people on the bus.

Jack walked toward the middle. The middle seemed like a safe place. To his left, three rows back, an old woman sat with a plastic scarf over her perm. She looked up at him as he passed and crossed herself. That was unnerving, he thought. It made him think of *Dracula*, when Harker boards the wagon that takes him to the castle. Or maybe it was just because he looked so bad, trudging through the rain all morning.

Sitting down, he knew better. That old woman had seen something in his eyes. Something hunted. Something very afraid.

Staring out the window, he watched the suburbs roll past. Street upon street of medium-sized houses. Medium-sized houses in a medium-sized town. All of them were virtually the same save the paintjob and the landscaping. Then an idea struck him.

Wherever Mr. Grin and Gina were, it most probably wasn't in one of these houses. That would be too risky. He had heard her scream, loud and piercing. That would arouse some kind of suspicion in a neighborhood like this. In a neighborhood like the one Tim Fox lived in. Of course, that was assuming Tim Fox was home. He might not be. He might be Mr. Grin. Jack tried to match the Mr. Grin he saw in his mind with the younger Tim Fox he'd seen in pictures. There was maybe something familiar there, like his mind was trying to find someone. Like it was *really close* to finding someone, but he couldn't come up with a place. Couldn't come up with a name.

The bus went through its stops and Jack sat in the seat, tension tightening his neck, throbbing in his temples.

By the time the bus reached its fifth stop, he almost had himself convinced it wasn't even worth bothering Tim Fox. It was a stupid idea. He was part of Gina's past. Probably never even thought about her anymore. And he may not even want to give the time of day to the man who had quite possibly taken Gina from him.

The bus made its fifth stop and he stood up, wanting to run, wanting to continue through the day as fast as he possibly could. He stepped out into the cold, drawing it into his lungs. It almost felt welcome after the cramped steaminess of the bus.

FOURTEEN

On his way to Tim Fox's, Jack worked out what he would say. It was an admittedly strange way to approach someone. He would have to say just the right things in order for the man to even let him in his house.

And what if Tim Fox *is* Mr. Grin? What then?

He didn't know. Would the bloodshed start right away? Would Tim Fox try and hide the fact he was Gina's captor? All these things seemed so abstract to Jack that he had a hard time thinking about them.

He walked up the steps leading to the front door and took a deep breath. Reaching out, he knocked on the worn wood of the door.

The man who opened the door was not what he was expecting at all. The only pictures he'd seen were headshots, nearly ten years old. Maybe it was the same with every guy, but he pictured Tim Fox as either a threatening musclebound jerk or a totally hideous beast. Someone so pitiable as to make him wonder how Gina could have ever gone out with him or someone so perfectly masculine as to make him think the only reason Gina would have broken up with him was if he was some kind of violent lunatic.

Tim Fox was neither of these things. He seemed a lot older than Gina. The first signs of gray were starting at the temples of his otherwise sand-colored hair. He had a short beard, also flecked with bits of white. He wore a pair of stylish, round plastic-frame glasses. He looked like he could have been a college professor or perhaps a psychologist. Jack didn't know if Gina had ever said what it was he did for a living. It also occurred to him that maybe this wasn't Gina's Tim Fox. After all, it couldn't be that uncommon of a name.

"Can I help you?" Fox said. He raised his eyebrows when he spoke, a gesture Jack always found condescending. He looked tired.

"Maybe," Jack said, deciding to just launch into his story before this guy could raise serious questions about him. "My name is Jack Orange. You don't know me but I believe you used to know my girlfriend, Gina Black."

At this his face lit up a little bit, the way a person's will when they think about someone they haven't thought about for a long time.

"Yes, Gina . . ." Then his look grew immediately concerned. "Is she okay?"

"Well, I hope so," Jack said. "Although, I was wondering if I could ask you a few things about her."

Fox glanced back into the house.

Jack's heart skipped a beat.

Was he hiding something? Was that what that look meant?

"I guess you should come in out of the rain," he offered. "But we'll have to keep our voices down. I just put the baby down for her nap."

"This shouldn't take very long."

"Come on in." His voice was low, soothing. Jack supposed Gina had felt a great sense of comfort when around this man. Then he remembered she had ultimately left him because he was fucking someone else.

Jack followed Tim through the living room and into the kitchen at the back of the house.

Tim pulled out a wooden chair and gestured for Jack to sit down. "Can I get you something to drink?" he asked.

"No, but thanks."

Tim pulled out the chair across from Jack, sat down, crossed his legs, and said, "So what's up?"

"I know you and Gina were together for quite a while. Believe me, I wish there was someone else I could bother with this but I know that no one knows another person like a lover. They're the ones that see just about every side of a person. Especially all the really ugly sides."

Tim furrowed his brow but nodded at the same time. "I think I'd have to agree with you. Are you sure Gina's okay?"

"Well, physically, I guess, she's fine. I was just kind of wondering if she ever seemed, I don't know . . . *dang*erous to you?"

"Gina was certainly an interesting woman. She had a few different sides. You probably know that."

"I'm afraid maybe this goes beyond that. To be honest with you, she's in the wellness center."

"Really?" He sounded genuinely surprised. "Any particular reason?"

"I think she's delusional. And she's developed a drinking problem."

"Hmmm. I didn't know she touched the stuff." So he *did* know her. "As for the delusional part . . . I can see that."

"I'm just kind of wondering . . . and her doctor is just kind of wondering if it's just me or if these are patterns in her behavior. You know, has she been like this forever or is it just *me* making her crazy? I mean, was she ever violent when she was with you? Did she ever run off and not come back for days?"

"Let's see . . . Again, I couldn't really say about the drinking. When she was with me, she never touched the stuff but it's entirely possible she developed a taste for it. She always had a problem letting go. I don't recall her ever being violent and the only time she ran off was when she decided she was going to start sleeping at your place."

Jack lowered his head. Only a few minutes and Tim had already made him feel guilty. He didn't have time for guilt. He decided to trudge ahead with his line of questioning.

"But you said you could understand the delusional part. Did she ever have any delusions?"

"I don't know that I would call them delusions, really. She just . . . she just didn't think the way everybody else did. Did she ever take you to that field . . . with the trains?"

Immediately, it felt like Tim had stolen a vital part of their relationship. Jack nodded his head and scratched the idea of proposing to Gina there.

"Well, she called that 'When Two Worlds Collide.' Like it was a painting that needed a title or something. So we would stand in that freight car." A little grin played at the corner of his mouth. "Well, if you've been there with her, then you know it wasn't just *standing* we were doing. Anyway, she said that if you were to go through the freight car . . . like out the other side? You would find yourself in a different world entirely. So I was always coaxing her to do this. I would do it myself. Just to tease her, you know. Hop out on the far side of the freight car and then hop back in." He spread out his arms. "Still here. I'm still here, Gina, I would tell her. But she was terrified. Refused to do it herself. Said she was afraid if she went out then she wouldn't be coming back. I always thought that was a little bit odd."

Tim's back was to the refrigerator. Jack's back was to the opening of the living room. He heard a shuffling noise and was immediately on his feet. Tim had mentioned a baby. Jack didn't think a baby could be creeping up behind him. Tim stood up with Jack, his eyes full of alarm.

Jack turned around to see a blond girl who couldn't have been more than sixteen.

She wore a white button-down dress shirt, cuffed at the arms, her nipples erect against its fabric.

"Who's this, Timmy?" she asked.

Jack turned back to look at Tim. He guessed old habits were hard to break. Tim wore an embarrassed grin, clasping his hands in front of his chest.

"Jack," he said. "This is Amber. Amber, this is Jack. An old friend."

Jack guessed that old friends were rare for Tim. When compared to Amber, Jack certainly *felt* old. Knowing the time for useful information had passed, Jack said, "Thanks for your time, Tim," and started to leave the house.

From behind him, Tim screamed and Jack heard him drop to the ground.

The girl squealed and rushed to his side.

Nearly at the front door, Jack turned around and headed back into the kitchen, already knowing why Tim was screaming.

Collapsed on the linoleum of the kitchen, a wild look in his eyes, he clawed at his left forearm beneath his sweater. Amber held his right arm. Jack couldn't tell if she was trying to yank him up from the floor or if it was a gesture of comfort. Tim yanked the sleeve of his sweater up and looked, horrified, at what Jack already knew was there.

The strange mark.

Jack now stood over Tim.

"What's that?" Jack asked, playing ignorant. "Can I take a look?"

Tim continued to scream, his eyes darting around in his head. He pointed at Jack and screamed, "You have to leave! Amber! Get him out of the house!"

"I just need to see," Jack said. He felt sadistic, leaning over this man, trying to grab his arm so he could have a closer look. Already, since leaving Maria, he had nearly forgotten what the mark looked like. When he saw it on Tim's arm he realized he hadn't forgotten at all. Because he could identify this as the very same mark. The design was just so simple it wasn't something the mind wanted to dwell on.

Tim batted at him with his arm, trying to smack him away. Jack had seen everything he needed to see.

"Okay okay," he said. "I'm going. Sorry to bother you."

"Get the fuck out!" Tim shouted. And then, "You'll never find her! I hope you know that! You'll never find her!"

This did something to Jack's insides. This man was not like Maria. He was not a friend. By him being Gina's former lover, he was more like an enemy. Jack doubled back into the kitchen one final time. He put his foot on Tim's chest, forcing his back to the floor. Then he leaned over the frightened man and said, "I'm going to find her. Nothing is going to stop me from finding her. And if I find out you had anything to do with this . . . If I find out you hurt her in any way and caused her to do this, I'm coming back for you. So you might want to think about that." Then he poked the strange brand on Tim's arm, undoubtedly sending a shot of pain through him. "I hope you enjoy the gift."

Once again, Jack turned to leave the house, this time certain he would not be turning back. Tim continued to wail, his teenage girl cooing to him, telling him he was going to be all right, telling him to calm down, asking him if he needed to go to the hospital.

Jack banged out the door and into the gloom, surveying the little neighborhood, unfolding his map to figure out which direction he needed to go in order to find Sam's house. His head was as cloudy as the sky but, somehow, things made more sense now.

It was the mark. The brand. The tattoo. Whatever the hell it was. Maybe it was a clue. Whatever it was, it unified everything. So far it was the only thing that followed him through the day. Mr. Moran had the mark. He too had tried to attack Jack. Maria had the mark and she had not tried to attack him but maybe that was only because she knew him better than the others. And then Tim had received the mark. He had not really tried to attack Jack but he was in a big hurry to get him out of the house. Jack remembered what Maria had said about the mark. About how she had seen a clear picture of Jack in her head and he wondered if the others had seen the same thing. Was that why they were so eager to either attack him or run him out of the house? It was entirely possible. It would make sense if that were the case. Something like Pavlovian conditioning. You experience great pain and you associate someone with that pain then you probably will not want to see that person, afraid they may cause you pain.

He thought about taking the bus again but knew he didn't have any miracle change left in his pocket. He hoped that another miracle would surface, something that didn't come in a form as petty as correct change. Time was running out. It was now nearly two o'clock. Jack wondered how Gina was doing. He wasn't going to fool himself into thinking Mr. Grin was beyond hurting her. He had heard the screams. He knew Mr. Grin had stripped Gina down. Those things alone were enough to make Jack want to hurt him very badly. But, he reminded himself, he wasn't just going to have to hurt him. He was going to have to kill him. What would Mr. Grin have to do in order to make Jack feel comfortable about killing him?

No. Jack knew it wasn't about being comfortable with killing him. He didn't know if anyone outside of gang members and the military ever felt comfortable with killing another human being. But what would it take to make him *want* to kill Mr. Grin?

It was hard to think beyond his need to find Gina and take her to safety. To bring her back home.

He quickened his pace. On his way to Sam's house.

FIFTEEN

It was like the more things that happened to him, the more confused he became. Was he any closer to Gina now than he was when he had received his first call from Mr. Grin? He didn't know. He couldn't know. It just didn't seem possible. Of course, none of this seemed possible. It was like it was happening to someone else. He nearly resigned himself to the fact Mr. Grin was just toying with him. Like maybe they were states away by now. Maybe there really wasn't any hope at all of Jack finding them.

Then what happened?

Would tomorrow morning roll around and then . . . would that be it? Would that be the last he would ever hear of Gina?

No. He was going to find her. He *had* to find her.

As he walked at his now customary brisk pace through the neighborhood, maybe only a mile from Sam's house, his thoughts returned to the marks.

They had to mean something.

What did they mean?

Were they given to those people as a warning? As some way to dissuade them from helping Jack? If Mr. Grin were capable of somehow telepathically inflicting these marks on people he was a lot more powerful than Jack could have ever imagined. That was something bordering on the supernatural and, thus far in his life, Jack had never seen anything even remotely resembling the supernatural. Growing up in Glowers Hook, there had been rumors but, even there, he had not seen so much as a ghost. Not even something fleeting past the corner of his eye. What he had witnessed so far, both the good and the bad, could be explained through science or human nature.

On the other hand, maybe the marks were put there to help guide Jack. To show him he was on the right path. Admittedly, that was no less supernatural but he liked thinking Mr. Grin didn't hold all the cards.

His phone vibrated in his pocket. He couldn't remember turning it to the vibrate setting.

He pulled it out, holding it in the palm of his hand. There was a moment of dread before he flipped it open. But there was also a moment of joy. Because, as long as Mr. Grin was calling him, that meant the game was still being played. It was entirely possible, Jack thought, some third party would be onto Mr. Grin, stepping in to interrupt him from torturing Gina. What would happen then?

Finally flipping it open, he stared at it like it was some magical instrument.

He put the phone to his ear, not saying anything, continuing to walk, his legs moving in a rhythm they had established long ago.

A strange sloshy sound came from the other end. But no voices yet. This continued for nearly a minute, Jack's breath and heartbeat sounding just as loud in his ears.

Then: "Hear that?"

He didn't say anything. He did not want to play this psycho's game.

"I said, '*Hear that*!'" Mr. Grin shouted.

"Yeah, yeah. I heard it. What the fuck was it?"

"That was the sound of my dick in Gina's mouth."

Jack felt his gorge rise. But what could he do?

Nothing.

The only thing he could do was try to find her. Anything he said to Mr. Grin could only set him more off balance than he already clearly was.

"You like that sound?" Mr. Grin said. "Remember when she used to suck your dick? Let me tell you, you were lucky if it felt anything at all like this. Don't worry though, she's not going to bite it off or injure me in any way. I know you would be disappointed if the game couldn't continue. But, like I said, don't worry. She ain't gonna do nothin' with this gun at her head."

The sloshing sounds filled Jack's ear again. He heard Gina gag and then cough and then Mr. Grin's voice, not into the phone, saying, "Come on, you can take it. Suck it down in there." The picture came to Jack, unwanted, of Gina down on her knees, Mr. Grin holding the phone down near her mouth with his left hand, his right hand gripping a gun, pressing it to Gina's temple.

Maybe he could use this unwanted scene, though. Think about the background. Where are they?

In his imagination, the room was dim. Not dark, because it was light outside and maybe there were curtains or blinds drawn but it was never enough to keep out all the light. He saw a room that was not filthy but not clean and a little out of date. In the background, he saw a bland nightstand, bland lamp, and bland painting hanging up on the wall.

He realized he was picturing a hotel room. It had to be. Not that his imagination was the truth. But it was something so much greater than the nothing he had received so far.

The spitty sloshing sounds continued. He tried his hardest not to picture Gina.

He wanted to hang up. He didn't want to hear this. He looked forward to meeting Mr. Grin. No amount of physical pain the man could inflict on him would come even remotely close to this. This was degradation. It hurt his soul and he couldn't even imagine what it was doing to her.

"Now Jack," Mr. Grin said. "I'm gonna give you a choice. I can either come in her mouth, on her face, or on her tits. Which do you prefer?"

"What kind of choice is that?" he asked before he could even catch himself. The easiest thing, he knew, was to play his game but he couldn't let go that much. He couldn't give that much to this man.

"There is, of course, a fourth choice. If you choose to answer none of the above then I can ram this gun up her asshole and unload. Then I can unload myself into one of the hot exit wounds. *Answer me, you little fuck!"*

"On her chest," Jack whispered into the phone, looking to his left at the row of sane little houses, wondering if anyone who saw him could possibly imagine what kind of conversation he was having.

"On her what? I couldn't hear you so well. Kind of hard to concentrate."

"On her chest."

"Chest. Well, you got a chest and I got a chest but Gina here, she got tits. I can't hold it much longer, shit crawler."

"On her tits, okay, fucking come all over her tits. Is that what you want me to say?"

"That's exactly what I wanted you to say. But I changed my mind. I want to come in her mouth. Make her suck it all down. That way if you do find me and kill me, the next time you kiss her, you can imagine all my little sperms down there in her stomach."

Mr. Grin's voice was hitching and Jack knew he was doing exactly what he said he was doing.

The phone went back to the sloshing/gagging sounds.

Mr. Grin's voice, from far away again, "Jacky here wanted me to go on your tits but you're swallowin' it, baby."

There was another gag and then some slapping sounds.

Jack learned the art of walking with his eyes closed. If he had to keep them open, if he had to see all the sane lives around him, he might be forced to go up to one of their doors and see if they could help him make his life sane too.

He heard a final gag, more slapping, and then something that could have been vomiting.

"I certainly feel better now," Mr. Grin said.

Jack, for lack of anything better to say, said, "I know where you are," and flipped the phone shut, sliding it back into his pocket like the more quickly he put it away the more quickly he put that horrible image out of his head. His eyes still closed, he pictured the scene. Mr. Grin and Gina slowly faded from the room and he tried to think about all the hotels in Alton.

He opened his eyes as the phone vibrated in his pocket. He wasn't going to answer it this time. For now, he had surpassed all he could take. In his head, he apologized to Gina if Mr. Grin was going to take this out on her. But, Jack knew, if he had to hear that man right now, he was going to do something that just might spoil everything.

The rain started up again and made everything even colder.

He put his hands in his pockets, drawing into himself, and continued walking.

SIXTEEN

Sam Black lived on the edge of the suburbs, where it became just a little bit seedy. Apartments and duplexes mostly, mixed in with fly-by-night storefronts—check cashing places, tanning salons, restaurants. All likely to be out of business this time next year, leaving the space vacant or occupied with some other evanescent business.

Sam lived in a two-story split level. He lived on the first floor. Jack had hung out with Sam a few times and had heard a lot about him from Gina. As far as she knew, he had not had sex since he was sixteen. He worked in a video store a few days a week and, when not working, spent most of his time smoking pot in front of the television and watching porn, movies most people had never heard of, playing video games, or reading comic books. Sam was sloth personified. Jack liked him quite a bit.

Jack tapped on his living room window. Sam's blinds were drawn and Jack hoped he was home. He had to knock on the window because if he knocked on the front door then one of the residents from upstairs would undoubtedly come down and open it. He didn't want to disturb them. It was easier and more immediate to just knock on the window.

He slid his phone out of his pocket.

2:46.

He had wasted a lot of time walking here. And he didn't really know how Sam could possibly help him.

A bloodshot eye peered out between two parted slats of the blind.

Then a hand appeared, holding up the index finger. One second. Then the index pointed to the left. Front door. He had become accustomed to these hand signals.

He walked up the porch steps and stood at the front door.

Sam pulled the door open. He wore an old Cincinnati Bengals shirt and baggy, dirty pajama pants. His salt and pepper hair was pulled back into a thin, greasy-looking ponytail.

"Jack," he said, opening the door. Jack was greeted as much by the smell of smoke and sweat and possibly old semen as he was by his name.

"Sam."

"Come in. Come in." Sam ushered him inside.

The door to his apartment was to the left. Jack followed him into the smelly pit.

If he told Sam Gina was missing, could he trust him not to tell anyone else?

He thought he could trust Sam.

And Sam couldn't tell anyone else if he came along with Jack. This was what he was hoping for. He didn't know if he was putting him in danger or not. He didn't feel any sense of pressing danger. And if he sent Sam away before they came to Mr. Grin, *if* they came to Mr. Grin, then there wouldn't be any harm done.

"Sit down." Sam tossed a blanket from the couch and gestured for Jack to sit down. Jack did, feeling a little dirty as he nestled into the once-off-white-now-more-brown cushions. The television was paused. A woman was in between two men, one of them fucking her mouth, the other fucking her from behind. A band of static ran through the middle of the screen. Jack found that he did not want to look at it. Thankfully, Sam grabbed the remote and turned the power off.

"Sorry 'bout that."

"It's okay."

"I just get so used to being alone I forget what I'm doing sometimes. Everything okay?"

"Not really."

"You're soaked," he observed. "You walk here?"

"Yeah."

"What happened to the car?"

"It's a long story. It's all a pretty long story."

"Gina okay?"

"No, Sam, I don't think she's okay at all."

"Are you serious?"

"I am. Things are . . . well, they're really fucked. That's what they are. They just haven't been right since this morning."

"You going to tell me what happened?"

"Yeah, I'll tell you. Although I don't think I'm supposed to. Before I start though, let me give you a warning. In a few minutes, you're going to feel a very intense pain in your left arm. No, you're not going to have a heart attack. But you will be left with some kind of brand. And when you're having these pains, you're going to see a picture of me in your head. I want you to remember what I'm doing in this picture. I think the pain will go away. But I'm not sure."

Sam stared at him, digesting everything. Jack knew Sam was a smart guy, it just took a moment for reality to penetrate through the layers of chemicals usually surging through his body.

"If you say you're serious," he said. "I believe you. I should probably start numbing the pain then, huh?"

He sat down beside Jack and grabbed a water bong from a table beside the couch. It must have been packed and ready to go. He put his lips to it and held a lighter to the bowl on the other side. Once he had sucked a good lungful, he offered it to Jack.

"No, thanks."

"That's right. I forgot. You don't do this, do you?"

"Not in a while."

"You're missing out."

"I've heard."

"So," he hissed as he exhaled a plume of smoke. "Where's Gina?"

"I don't know."

"You don't know? She run off or something?"

"Has she done that before? Run off?"

He inhaled again. "Not that I know of. Not when she was living at home anyway. I think when she was dating Tim Fox, she might have ran off a couple of times. Came here to just chill out after a fight or something or . . ."

"Or what?"

"Well, there were a couple times I know of—like after she knew that shit was fucking around on her—when she would go out with some friends and pick up a guy. Just to, you know, fuck him out of spite or something."

Jack was kind of surprised. If this had happened, she hadn't told him anything about it.

"She did this a lot?" he asked.

"No. Not a lot. Like I said, just a couple times maybe. I told her she shouldn't do that. A lot of girls end up getting hurt that way. Hurt or catching some kind of disease." Sam shook his head, inhaled again.

"Do you know if she had any stalkers or anything like that?"

"No. I don't think so. Gina didn't really let guys down easy. Once she was finished with them, they didn't really have any interest in her."

"Why's that?"

"She just doesn't let them down easy, that's all."

Jack wondered if that's what this was. Could it be? Could she have grown tired of him and concocted this whole thing just to make him want absolutely nothing to do with her? It was possible, he guessed. Hell, *anything* was possible. But this was Gina, *his* Gina. They loved each other. He didn't think she would do anything like that to him.

"So what's been goin' on?" Sam asked.

Jack told him. He told him as quickly as possible but tried not to leave anything out. Even the smallest detail that meant nothing to him might mean something to Sam. All the while, he was conscious of the time slipping through his fingers.

Sam sat back on the couch, completely stoned, his eyes barely open, listening to it all.

When Jack was finished, Sam said, "That is *fucked up*!"

Then he screamed. Threw himself off the couch and onto the floor, his right hand wrapped around his left wrist, his girth covering both of his arms like he was trying to put out some kind of fire.

Jack went to him, kneeling down beside him as Sam flopped on the cluttered floor. Jack put his arm across Sam's shoulders.

"It's okay," he said, trying to comfort him. "Just hang on."

"*Oh Jesus fuck!*" he shouted. He was now doubled up, his forehead resting on the floor, his knees pulled up into his ample stomach.

Jack held him tighter.

Sam suddenly uncoiled himself, pushing against Jack, forcing him onto the couch.

Sam's eyes were full of rage. Jack saw the brand on his arm. This one was bloody, as though they had gained intensity. Or maybe it was because pain was the object of the mark and since Sam had undergone efforts to dull the coming pain, the mark had to be a little fiercer, a little more violent.

"*Get the fuck out of here!*" he roared.

"It's okay, Sam. It's just me, Jack."

"*What did you do to her! What did you do to her, you sick fuck!*"

"Nothing!" Jack shouted, feeling defensive. Sam had it all wrong. Jack was trying to *help* Gina. He would never hurt her.

Sam grabbed the heavy bong from the table. Jack stood up, backing away toward the door.

"Don't," Jack said.

"You're not getting away." Sam raised the bong over his head.

Before Jack could even attempt to leave the apartment or get out of the way, the bong was hurling at him, shattering against his shoulder, cutting through his shirt.

"Fuck!"

Maybe he *should* run. Just get the hell away from the suddenly raging Sam as fast as he could. But he was tired of running. If he just left it at this then he wouldn't have got what he came here for, which was Sam's help.

"Help me!" he shouted. "Help me find her, Sam!"

"I'm not helping you do anything."

Sam crossed the room toward Jack, dragging comic books beneath his feet. He clasped his large hands around Jack's shoulders.

"Get away from the fucking door. You're not going anywhere."

He threw Jack into the middle of the room, into the coffee table.

That one hurt. The wood dug into his back.

Sam stood over him, kicking at him. Jack rose up and lunged at Sam's knees. He put everything into it and managed to force him back and then down onto the floor. It probably helped that Sam was so stoned. Otherwise, Jack didn't see how he could possibly take him down.

Sam landed a punch to the side of Jack's head. Everything washed red and black before he landed his own punch in the middle of Sam's face. He didn't like the way Sam's nose felt under his knuckles. Popping and spewing forth blood.

Jack stood up. Sam quickly stood up right behind him. He swung his meaty left arm at Jack. Jack grabbed the wrist and yanked downward, catching Sam off balance.

Again Sam was on the floor.

And Jack was on top of him again. This time he went for the left arm. He held it extended against the floor.

He clapped his palm down on the brand.

It was hot, nearly burning his hand. He felt the raised pattern beneath his palm. He made a fist, trying to grab at the brand.

Beneath him, Sam winced. He bucked his hips trying to throw Jack from him. But Jack was small and wiry, not able to be bucked off so easily.

Jack pulled his hand away from Sam's arm.

And the brand was gone.

He held his own hand out in front of him.

He opened it, looking down into the palm.

The brand was there. Part of Sam's flesh lay in the palm of his hand.

Sam no longer bucked beneath him.

Slowly, Jack got off him, collapsing on the couch.

Sam continued to lie in the middle of the floor, taking long deep breaths. His left arm sprawled limply beside his head. There was a rectangular absence of skin where the brand once was. Blood flowed freely from it.

Sam's eyes were closed.

"What the fuck was that?" he said.

"I don't know," Jack said.

"Jesus, I wanted to *kill* you."

"You don't want to kill me anymore?"

"No. You're Jack. Why'd I want to kill you?"

"I don't know. Why *did* you want to kill me?"

"The pain. God, I've never felt pain like that. Did you get that thing off me?"

"Yeah, I did." Jack held it up. Sam opened his eyes and looked at it.

"You were right. I had a picture of you in my head when I felt that."

"What was I doing?"

"You were doing things to Gina."

"Like what?"

"Cutting her. Fucking her. Cutting and fucking her."

"You know I'd never hurt Gina, right, Sam? You know that, don't you?"

"Yeah. You're the best guy she's ever had. By far. I know you wouldn't hurt her."

"Then why did you see that . . . in your head?"

"I don't know. It was like, for a minute there, I didn't have any control over my thoughts at all."

"I want to try and find Gina, Sam. Will you help me?"

"Like come with you?"

"Yeah. Will you come with me?"

"I'd do anything for my sister. If you think she's in danger, I'll come with you."

SEVENTEEN

It was well after three o'clock by the time they managed to raise Sam
from the floor. Jack had put the brand/hunk of Sam's skin on a
glossy *Spider-Man* comic spread out on the coffee table. Once Sam
was upright, he said, "I'm gonna go to the bathroom and get cleaned
up a little bit."

"Okay," Jack said. Sam was a mess. Blood coated his face from
where Jack had punched him. He figured it was highly likely he had
broken Sam's nose. He was sorry about it but knew it was all done
in self-defense and there were a lot worse things than a broken nose.
Then there was the matter of the missing skin on his forearm. It was
definitely going to turn into a scar. While it was bloody, it didn't seem
to go down that deep. It was kind of like the outer layer of a blister
had been pulled off.

With Sam in the bathroom, Jack picked up the brand, holding it
delicately in his fingertips and sitting back on the stinky couch.

What the hell was it?

No longer did he think the mark was on his side. Now he thought
the mark was given to people to make them turn against him. To
hinder him in his quest. Jesus, just thinking like that made him feel
like he was going insane. A quest. He didn't have a quest yesterday.
Yesterday was a Saturday and he was just a guy like a million other
guys who dreaded going into work on Monday. Today he would
have been content to just sit around the house on his one day off
and enjoy the company of his girlfriend. His girlfriend who he was

going to make his fiancée.

Now that had all been blown to hell.

This was how he was spending his day off.

A day he would have hoped to remember as the day he proposed to Gina. Now he would remember it as the day he either won or lost Gina.

The brand had come away just as it was on Sam's arm. That is, only the lines of the brand came away. That rectangle with the horizontal line through it.

Jack thought it had to mean something. It seemed to be some kind of design, almost like a logo. If it was just meant to inflict pain and keep people away from him then he figured it could have been a less intricate mark like a simple slash or "X" or something. But this looked like it was trying to be some kind of stylized symbol.

Maybe Sam would have an idea where to look for her.

Absently, Jack stared at the brand until Sam emerged from the bathroom, his face wiped clean and a bandage applied to his arm. Then he slid the brand into his pants pocket.

"Ready," Sam said.

"Do you have any ideas where she might be?"

"Not really. You already check with her friends?"

"I don't really think she's with her friends. The phone calls, remember? And I was with her right before she went missing. I did talk to Maria though, from the coffee shop?"

"Oh, yeah, Maria. Hadn't seen her?"

"No. Didn't have any ideas at all, really. She got branded too."

"Did she try and kill you?"

"No. I think I left before she could really get the urge. And I think she wants to sleep with me."

"Have your babies, huh?"

"Gross."

"So . . . no ideas?"

"Well, not any legitimate ones. I mainly just feel like we should keep moving, you know. I don't know that it's doing any good just to sit around talking about it, but at the same time, if we keep moving and we're going in the wrong direction, then that's not going to help a lot either."

"How much time do you have?"

"Basically until tomorrow morning."

"And then?"

"It's over, I guess. Either someone dies or he takes Gina away."

"That's like kidnapping, isn't it?"

"Yeah, but I can't call the police. He said he would know if I called the police and he would just finish her right there."

"I'd like to get my hands on that guy."

"I'd like to know who the fuck it is. I did have one idea . . ."

"What's that?"

"I think maybe he took her to some kind of hotel or motel."

"Yeah? Why's that?"

"Just kind of a hunch."

"Well, Alton's got plenty of those."

"Do you know of most of them?"

"I think most of them are up by the highway."

"I'm thinking it almost has to be one that isn't really populated, you know?"

"Well, I don't really know about that. I don't know how full they're going to be on a Sunday morning. This *is* Alton, you know. There isn't much of a reason for people to be here unless they're just passing through. I'm guessing most of the truckers and the business-types check out early. If they would be here on a Sunday morning at all. And really, what are a few screams coming from a hotel room, anyway? Someone overhears them, as long as they aren't too pro-longed or desperate-sounding, and they just dismiss it as laughter or sex or something else."

"That's kind of what I'm afraid of."

"We'll find her," Sam said.

"You have a car, right?"

"You're going to use me for my car?"

"It would help a lot."

"Yeah, I've got a car. You want to go up by the highway?"

"I guess that's a good place to start."

"Let me get the keys."

Sam disappeared into the kitchen to get the keys. He came back, turning off lights as he did so, and Jack followed him through the front door.

A cop car was in the driveway.

Jack's heart lurched. His first thought was that the cop was here to tell them something terrible had happened to Gina. His second thought was the cop was here to put a bullet through each of them. To punish Jack for getting Sam's help.

The cop got out of the driver's side and raised his arm, "Can you two stay right there?"

Jack and Sam both stopped, stupidly raising their hands above their heads.

"Do you live on the ground floor?" the cop asked.

"I do," Sam said. He nodded toward Jack, keeping his hands raised. "He doesn't live here."

"There was a complaint about some noise. The caller said it sounded like there was a fight going on. Were you two fighting?"

"No, sir," Sam said. "We were watching a movie. Maybe I had the TV up too loud."

The cop moved closer to them. He looked at Sam and said, "What happened to your nose?"

It was bulbous and purple.

Sam laughed it off. "I wish I knew."

"What kind of answer is that?" the cop asked.

"Unfortunately, it's the only one I can give. Some of my friends took me out last night. I'm afraid I had a little too much to drink and when I woke up this morning I found I had this little souvenir."

"Regardless, I think I'd better come in and take a look around."

"I kind of need to get my friend here to work . . ." Jack knew this was a mistake as soon as Sam began. It made it sound like he was hiding something.

"Shouldn't take long," the cop said, already approaching the apartment. "You guys can put your arms down."

Jack and Sam followed the cop to the apartment. Jack couldn't begin to fathom the ridiculousness of this. Here was a cop not two feet away from them. How easy it would be to just say, hey look, I've got this situation … And tell him everything. The idea almost sounded good to Jack. If what Mr. Grin had said was true. If *Jack* called the *police*, then maybe Mr. Grin would know because his connection was the dispatcher or something. But if the police were already *here* then how could Mr. Grin possibly know if Jack told them anything?

Unless it was Mr. Grin who sent the cop here in the first place.

If he's capable of supernaturally branding people then maybe he's capable of knowing what's going on.

Jack and Sam hovered around the cop as he went through the apartment. Luckily, the bong was all smashed on the ground so it wasn't immediately recognizable as a bong. Sam kicked the golden metal bowl part of it under the end table. Jack's mind raced. The cop took both their names. He got Jack's address, writing it down in his pad.

"This place is a wreck," the cop said.

"I know, officer," Sam said. "I drink a lot. But that's not a crime, is it?"

"The kitchen smells like spoiled milk."

"On top of being a drunk, I'm also very lazy."

"I'm starting to not like your attitude," the cop said.

"I apologize, officer."

Jack was starting to wish Sam would stop. He was going to end up getting them ticketed or dragged to the station for something completely stupid. Jack stayed close by them as they went from room to room, simultaneously making sure Sam didn't say anything too incriminating and watching the cop.

It was possible, Jack thought, that *this* cop was Mr. Grin's connection to the force. If that was the case, and Jack couldn't even believe he was thinking of this, he could take the cop out. Take him captive or something and force the cop to tell him where Gina was. But that would be an extremely bold move. If it didn't work exactly the way Jack wanted it to, he could find himself in jail or even dead, shot by the cop in so-called self-defense.

He found himself looking at the cop, thinking he was just stalling them, but also looking at his gun hanging in his belt, the police radio, hanging at the ready on his shoulder.

Between him and Sam, it was possible the cop could be taken down and restrained.

Jack's phone vibrated in his pocket. Reaching in to take it out, the cop whirled, immediately stopping what he was doing, his hand already on his gun.

"It's just my phone," Jack said. "Is it okay to take it?"

"I guess," the cop said.

Jack flipped the phone open, walking back into the living room. Jack had planned to put it on speakerphone the next time Mr. Grin called so Sam could hear what he sounded like. Maybe Sam would be able to identify him from the voice. But he couldn't do that now, even though he was tempted to. He could just keep it on speakerphone and let Mr. Cop hear everything Mr. Grin was doing to Gina. He remembered a feature on his phone that allowed him to record conversations and, before answering it, he pressed the button that activated the voice memo.

Jack flipped the phone open, hoping it was going to catch everything, and said, "Hello."

"My," Mr. Grin began. "That's the most pleasant introduction I've received all day. Wouldn't be because there's a cop going through your friend's house right now, would it?"

"How do you know that?"

"I told you. You don't want to go to the police."

"I didn't. I swear."

"Okay. I believe you."

Jack wanted to ask Mr. Grin if he had sent the cop here or if it really was just some strange coincidence but knew it wouldn't do any good.

"Just thought I'd call," Mr. Grin said. "To keep you updated. It's been a long time since I've fucked Gina, Jack. Thought you might want to hear it."

Jack wanted to say all kinds of things but managed to fight the urge and say nothing.

He heard the sound of Mr. Grin's phone shift and figured *he* must have been put on speakerphone.

He heard Gina wince . . . and speak.

"Jack. I love you. Oh, God, Jack, please find me. Please."

"Where are you?" Jack said casually into the phone. Of course, he knew Mr. Grin would probably kill her if she told him where they were.

"I can't tell you. Just . . . please."

Then he heard her breath coming in short bursts, skin slapping skin, Mr. Grin grunting from somewhere far away. Everything built to its strange rhythm, Gina's breaths so sharp it sounded like the phone was right next to her mouth. Mr. Grin grunted loudly and then the phone call ended. Jack looked at the phone as though it had somehow forsaken him.

He pressed buttons until he found an options menu. He scrolled down to the "Voice Memo" selection. He highlighted that one and clicked on it. The conversation was there in its entirety. He would let Sam listen to it if the ass didn't end up in jail. Maybe it would strike some sort of chord with him.

He was so full of fury and rage his thoughts turned back to the cop and he was almost ready to attack him, certain he would be able to tell him who Mr. Grin was, but he was already backing down the driveway. Timed perfectly. Everything seemed like it was timed so fucking perfectly.

Sam stood at the door to his apartment.

"He left in a fucking hurry," Sam said.

"Yeah."

"He was supposed to come back and breathalyze me."

"Breathalyze you?"

"Yeah, I guess that's what you get for telling cops you drink a lot. You know how I told him I was taking you to work? He wanted to make sure I was able to do it 'unimpeded' was how he put it."

"Then he just drove off."

"Well, he did ask about the blood in the bathroom. I told him I didn't know exactly but I thought it came from my nose or maybe my girlfriend was menstruating. Good thing he didn't see that hunk of skin you tore off me. Would have probably thought we were cannibals too."

"Do your neighbors complain a lot?"

"Huh?"

"Well, I mean, if someone complained it would have had to be the people above you, right?"

"Never really thought of that. I guess so. They're never here during the day, though."

"It *is* Sunday though."

"No. They go away most weekends. We could go up there but I doubt they're there right now."

"I don't think the cop was really investigating much of anything."

"No?"

"No. I think he was sent as a warning."

"We should have fucking taken him out."

"That's kind of what I had planned but now he's gone."

"I guess we should be gone too, huh?"

"The sooner the better."

It was 4:36.

EIGHTEEN

Sam fired up the car and the sound of the Misfits blasted from the aged and badly worn speakers. He made no attempt to turn it down. He backed out haphazardly into the road, seemingly unaware that any cars may be speeding toward him, and gunned the accelerator until they were out on the state route and headed toward the highway.

He ran red lights and stop signs, acting not at all like a person who has just had a run-in with the police.

Once they reached a straightaway, Jack turned down the volume on the stereo and pulled out his cell phone. He found the latest call and said, "I want you to listen to this and tell me if you recognize the guy's voice. It's a little disturbing. I just want to warn you."

"Give it here," he said.

Jack watched for his reaction as he held it up to his right ear, a cigarette burning in his left hand. Miraculously, he managed to keep control of the speeding car.

After a few seconds, a look of distaste crossed Sam's face and Jack almost thought he was going to throw the phone out the window. Instead, he angrily flipped it closed and tossed it over onto Jack's lap.

"I tell you . . . When we find that guy I'm gonna cut his balls off and chew on 'em a little bit."

"Did he sound at all familiar?"

"Shit. He sounded like every fat fuck I run into every day."

"Did you think . . ." Jack began. "Did you think it sounded like he was . . . *smiling?*"

"Yeah. A little." Sam plastered a smile on his face and mimicked some of what Mr. Grin said. "Yeah, I think it did sound like he was smiling. You know, there was this kid we went to school with. We all called him Smiley, you know, because it looked like he was always smiling. Maybe it was just the shape of his mouth or something."

Jack felt his hopes surge wildly out of control.

Was it possible?

"So, you think it could be him? What was his name?"

"Oh, his name was David Lattimore. It couldn't be him though. He killed himself shortly after graduation." Sam chuckled. "Maybe I'm sick but the only thing I could picture was him swinging from that rope with a smile plastered on his face. It must have been a fucking weird thing to see."

Jack picked the phone up from his lap and held it in his hand, not putting it away, cradling it, trying to draw some kind of answer from it.

Soon they reached the highway and Sam slowed down. It looked like every highway exit area on every interstate in America, lined with chain hotels, chain restaurants, and chain gas stations. Like the developers had dropped their pants and shat out what every mid-size city in America had.

"Where do you want to start?" Sam said.

Jack thought about it.

He didn't know.

Didn't have any ideas.

He realized what a monumental undertaking this would be. Not to mention the fact he had absolutely no idea what they were looking for. Could he just walk into the motels and ask if they had seen someone fitting Gina's description come in that morning?

He didn't think that would do a lot of good. If Mr. Grin had had a morning of torture planned for Gina then he probably wasn't going to go parading her through all the hotel lobbies. Most likely he would have left Gina restrained in the car while he did the checking in. Maybe he even worked at one of these hotels. And he thought it must be some sort of unwritten code of privacy that the hotel clerks only give information to police. After all, at least a fourth of people checking into hotels and motels were there to do something they probably wouldn't do in the comfort of their own home.

Sam pulled into the lot of a King's Castle.

"Here?" he asked.

Jack continued to look helplessly at his phone. Did he even want to begin looking here? What was the likelihood they would actually find her? And how much time would they waste going into each of these places?

"I don't know," Jack said. "Do you have any ideas at all?"

"I'm as lost as you are, Jack. Let me listen to that conversation again."

"Okay." He cued it up.

Again, Jack found himself looking at Sam while he listened to his sister being raped. This time, Sam's brow was furrowed in concentration.

Once finished, he pulled the phone away from his ear and handed it back to Jack.

"Listen to it again," he said. "I was trying to see if there was any kind of sounds that would give it away—you know, like the highway in the background or something? But I didn't hear any of that. But I think I heard something else. Towards the end, when she's panting or something, listen, and it almost sounds like she's trying to say something."

Jack couldn't listen to it fast enough. He started at the beginning and relistened to everything, paying close attention when it got to the end.

There was definitely some rhythm to her panting. Why would she be seductively panting in the first place? He figured if her mouth was uncovered, she would be screaming her head off unless she was someplace where she knew she wasn't going to be heard or unless she was trying to convey some sort of message without Mr. Grin's knowledge.

Jack started over and listened to it again.

He tried to verbalize what she may or may not have been trying to say.

"When . . . will . . . I . . . die?"

"Could be," Sam said.

"That doesn't make any sense."

"Yeah. It does seem like sort of a half-hearted musing for some-one in her situation."

"When . . . words . . . ride?"

"That's just dumb."

Jack started from the beginning, skipped straight to Gina's part.

It hit him hard. He felt his head spin. He thought he knew what she was trying to say.

"Turn around," he told Sam. "We're wasting our time up here."

Sam whipped the car around, all squealing rubber, and they tore out of the King's Castle parking lot, bolting across their lane and into oncoming traffic.

NINETEEN

Sam jerked the wheel to his right in order to avoid the oncoming traffic and ended up back in their own lane.

"So what did you hear?" he asked.

"I don't know if it'll make any sense to you," Jack said, his heart pounding away. "Where worlds collide."

"Huh?"

"Where worlds collide. Does that sound familiar?"

"Can't say it does."

"It's a place. Off of Groves Road. There's like this huge field there. But, more importantly, there are some train tracks where it looks like two engines have collided . . ."

"Ahhh. I know the place. It's where all of the teenagers go to smoke pot and drink and make-out. All that good stuff."

"Yeah. Well, Gina took me there once but I didn't know she had a name for it until I went to see Tim Fox this afternoon . . ."

"Her old boyfriend?"

"Yeah. Her old boyfriend."

"You really are serious about finding her."

"Anyway. He told me she called it 'When Two Worlds Collide'."

"But you didn't know she called it that?"

"No. I mean unless it was one of those things she just brought up that kind of . . . well, maybe I wasn't paying attention. I mean, if she mentioned it while we were actually there then there's a good chance I could have been thinking about other things . . ."

"Don't need to know any more about that. Thanks."

The sky darkened again. Lightning slashed the sky, gouging out the rain, pouring down, icy cold, onto the car.

"Piss," Sam said as the windows started fogging up. He flipped a dial to defrost and turned on the windshield wipers. Well, windshield wiper, anyway. Apparently, only the one on the driver's side worked. "That's new," Sam said. "So, you think that's where he took her. To that rail car?"

"I think, so far, it's the only thing that makes any sense at all. You know how to get there?"

"Definitely. You know, there's another place out there too—"

But he was cut off.

A car had whipped over from the oncoming lane, coming right for them. Sam slammed on the brakes but with all the rain and what were probably significantly undertreaded tires, it didn't do a lot of good. Jack braced himself for the impact.

A bright light exploded behind his closed eyes. He felt the seatbelt grab his shoulder. Wondered, panicked, if Sam was wearing his. Glass showered him. And, like that, it was over.

He sat still in his seat, afraid to move, conscious of the sudden silence of the car and the rain beating down outside the shattered passenger-side window. He looked over at the driver's side.

Sam wasn't there.

Shit, he thought. The stupid fucker wasn't wearing his seatbelt.

The car hissed steam from in front of him. Raindrops hammered his fevered skin. He had to find Sam. Had to make sure he was okay.

He undid his seatbelt with clumsy hands and stepped out into the rain.

"Look out!" someone shouted.

Jack had enough time to turn around before something hit him.

The something, someone, drove him onto the ground. He felt a cold pain open at his ribs.

Jesus, had the person cut him?

The person was now on top of him, snarling above him.

"Maria?" he said, completely confused.

Why was Maria holding him down on the ground? Why did Maria

have that knife in her hand?

"Never find her," Maria snarled.

This was definitely not the Maria he knew. Of course not, he thought. This was the Maria transformed by the mark. This was a dangerous Maria that he did not have the joy of sticking around in the coffee shop long enough to see.

She raised the knife above her head, preparing to drive it down.

He threw his arms up in front of his face, as though this would stop ten inches of sharpened steel.

He tried to throw her off, simultaneously preparing for the punch of steel into his skin.

It never came.

He felt the weight lifted from his hips.

Sam had her around the arms.

"Jesus," Jack said.

Sam was covered in blood. This was a lot worse than the bloody nose.

"We need to duct tape her and throw her in the trunk," Sam said.

Jack moved closer but out of Maria's reach. "Now," he said. "Why would we need to do that?"

"Just seems like the right thing to do."

"I've got another idea," Jack said. "We remove that brand there on her left arm and sweet little Maria goes back to being sweet little Maria. Does that sound like a better plan?"

"Can it involve duct tape?" Sam said. He really didn't look like someone who should be making jokes.

"What?" Jack said. "Do you have like a spare roll of duct tape in your car or something?"

"In the back. You can grab it." He strained with the force of holding Maria back.

Jack looked into the back seat of Sam's car. There had to be at least six rolls of duct tape there. He had no idea why Sam would need so much duct tape.

"Just don't let her go," Jack said.

Sam threw her against the car, trying to get her to drop the knife. She held strong. She bent her head over her shoulder, gnashing her teeth at Sam.

Grabbing the duct tape, Jack wondered where the police were now. For that matter, where were any concerned citizens? They were still on the state route. Their cars were bashed up in the middle of the road. Other cars were simply pulling around them. Jack certainly wasn't putting in any calls to the police. And, furthermore, he didn't want anyone to help them. If the police or an ambulance arrived here before they could get away then they would be forced to go to the hospital and fill out reports and other things that would undoubtedly burn away the rest of the night.

Had Mr. Grin planned this?

If he had planned the cop stopping by Sam's apartment, then it seemed very easy and logical he had planned this.

Jack grabbed a roll of duct tape and threw it, hard, at Maria's knife-wielding right arm.

She turned to him and snarled. He imagined that being a face she made when she was really into sex and wondered how, sometimes, very attractive people can become very ugly.

"We need to get the fuck out of here," he told Sam.

"We can't just leave her."

Jack threw another roll of duct tape, this time hitting the knife. It clattered to the ground.

"Hold her around the wrists," Jack told Sam.

Sam shifted his grip down. Jack approached them and Maria began kicking out wildly.

Jack put his back to her. Sam drove her to the asphalt, swaddling her in his girth.

Jack crouched down, feeling the immense pain in his ribs, and felt along her left arm.

He felt the brand raised under his fingertips. He grabbed a corner of it.

This one didn't come off as easily as Sam's had. It was like, over time, it had grown deeper roots or something.

Feeling time slip away, he realized he couldn't do a finesse job. He found the knife, lying on the road.

"Sorry," he said to Maria.

Holding the loose skin away from her arm, he ran the knife along the brand, shearing it off.

Maria howled in pain.

"We gotta go," Jack shouted. He heard sirens in the distance.

"We just gonna leave her here?"

"I guess we could take her with us."

Maria was sitting up on the asphalt now, staring down at her arm. Jack tucked the brand into her hand.

"Dude," Sam said. "I think she's in shock or something."

"Okay okay. Then we'll just leave her here and the ambulance will find her. She probably won't remember anything anyway. We just need to fucking go."

Sam trudged over to his car. He slid in behind the wheel and began cranking away at the engine. The engine didn't really crank at all.

"This thing's shit," Sam announced.

"Let's try hers."

"We're just gonna steal her car?"

"Why not? She stabbed me."

Jack slid into Maria's driver's seat. Her car was, actually, still running. The front wheels were not touching the ground, as it had run up on Sam's car. Sam jumped on the hood of his car, making Jack think of King Kong and, with a mighty heave, loosed the front of Maria's car.

Sam grabbed a roll of duct tape from the back of his car and hopped into the passenger side, banging the door shut. It met in the frame but didn't latch.

"Great, now I'm gonna have to hold the fucking thing," he said.

"You could always tape it shut," Jack said.

"Not a bad idea."

Jack whipped back into the traffic and gunned the car. Unfortunately, it wouldn't go faster than 35 mph. He guessed it was better than walking.

"That was fucking wild," Sam said. He was unspooling some of the tape, trying to fasten the door from the inside.

"To say the least," Jack said.

In the distance, a herd of sirens sped toward them.

"You better find some fucking back roads quick," Sam said.

Jack veered to his right, taking a street that went through the mall parking lot and ending in one of the upscale suburbs.

They were only about fifteen minutes from where they needed to be.

Jack drove along, wanting to go faster, and waiting to feel his phone vibrate in his pocket. Now seemed like an appropriate time for Mr. Grin to call.

TWENTY

Driving along, Jack found himself tense, waiting for the phone to vibrate. For once, he almost felt lucky no one else ever called him. That eliminated a lot of the suspense. Like he wouldn't have to jump when the phone went off only to look at the display and see that it was someone he knew. His parents called weekly, usually on Friday evening to see if he would be coming over at all that weekend. Other than that, Gina was the only person who called with any regularity. The phone sat in a cup holder in between him and Sam.

"She got you, huh?" Sam said, looking at the gash in Jack's side.

"Yeah."

"Hurt?"

"Not yet. It will." If I live until tomorrow, he thought.

"Wonder if she has anything in here to stop the blood?"

"It's a girl's car. There's gotta be something."

Jack thought of all the times Gina had borrowed the car. It seemed like, every time she got out of it, she left something behind. Notebooks, books, CDs, sweaters and coats (she claimed to get too hot when she was driving).

Sam turned around in his seat and went rummaging through the back.

"You don't look so great yourself," Jack said. "You're covered in blood."

"I think they're all surface wounds though. Nothing too deep. Maybe I nicked my head on some glass. Head wounds always bleed the most. Ah, here we go."

Sam brought a plastic package up from his explorations.

"What the hell's that?" Jack said.

"It's a package of pads. Must've been Maria's time of the month. Or maybe she just likes to be prepared. These are just *made* to absorb blood. And we've got some duct tape."

"Yeah," Jack said unenthusiastically. "Good thing you brought that along. Not embarrassing at all to go around with pads duct taped to you."

"Who are you really worried about impressing at this point?"

"I guess you're right."

"Okay. Now let me fix you. Just focus on driving."

Sam went about unwrapping one of the pads, unfolding it, and placing it on the gash in Jack's side.

"You might need to hold it right there for just a sec."

"Got it," Jack said, holding the pad in place.

Sam unspooled some duct tape and wrapped it around Jack's stomach. Jack was thankful for being virtually hairless.

"Too tight?" he asked.

"No. I think there's supposed to be some pressure in order to make the bleeding stop. Are you sure you're okay?"

"I'm not going to tape a bunch of pads to myself, if that's what you're trying to get me to do."

"Fine." *Let* me *be the one with pads strapped to him.*

Still no call. For the past few minutes, that was really all Jack could think about. As horrid as Mr. Grin's calls were, they at least let him know Gina was still alive. Mr. Grin could never call him again, he supposed, and the whole game might just end there. Would he be free to go to the police when the twenty-four hours were up? After knowing that Mr. Grin had some connection with the Alton police department, he didn't think he would ever feel comfortable calling 911 again. And he didn't think anything could be done with the FBI unless he first went through local law enforcement. Somehow, even if he went over their heads, he knew it would end up coming back to them.

"Hey," Jack said. "Before the crash, you were going to say

something about that place with the tracks . . ."

"Oh, yeah, if I remember correctly, there is actually a hotel back there. A *mo*tel really. Just one of those places you can drive up to your door, you know? The kind of place preferred by prostitutes and adulterers. A no-tell motel. Easy in. Easy out. Probably never asked for a driver's license or anything. But it's abandoned now. It's kind of creepy. And out in the middle of fucking nowhere. Still, though, I guess it should have probably been the first place I thought about when you mentioned a hotel."

"Maybe that's where she is."

"It's possible. We can get there from the tracks. We used to go there when we were in high school. Had some fine underage drinking parties there. It's off some out-of-the-way road but I think we could just cut through the Wilds and get there."

"The Wilds? Those are the woods on the other side of the tracks?"

"Yep. You're starting to learn your Alton geography, aren't you, Jack?"

"Reluctantly," he said.

The car began demonstrating a disconcerting bucking effort and Jack slowed it down even more. If there was one thing he had learned, it was that this car didn't like to exert itself. Probably not much before the crash and definitely not after it.

"I feel like we should have some kind of weapon or something," Jack said.

"Well, then I'm afraid it's time to thank friend Sam again," Sam said, plopping the huge knife Maria had used between them, right next to the cell phone. Jack figured it probably came from the cafe.

"I didn't even see you pick that up."

"Fat guy moves faster than light sometimes."

"Sam, if I make it through this I'm gonna buy you an ice cream cone."

"If *we* make it through this. She's my sister. I'm with you until the end."

"That makes me feel very good to hear," Jack said.

Then, out of nowhere, Sam said, "Did she ever tell you she's adopted?"

Jack didn't know how to respond to that. It probably would have had more of an effect if there were not such extenuating, much more serious things to deal with. People were adopted all the time. Especially now that it seemed like more twelve-year-olds were having kids themselves, coupled with the reality that no one wanted to take responsibility for anything anymore and people who were found to have abortions were called names like 'murderer'. The fact she didn't tell him did something to him. Of course, she could have just been sensitive about the subject and if, in the long run, it didn't matter anyway, he guessed it wasn't really important. Or, maybe . . .

"Does she know?" he asked Sam.

A look of bafflement crossed Sam's face. "I . . ." he stammered. "I couldn't really tell you. Don't know if I've ever even thought about it. I know I've never talked to her about it and my parents didn't introduce her as 'Their adopted daughter, Gina,' or anything. But . . . Well, I guess it's entirely possible she doesn't know. I was three when they found her so I know she was way too young . . ."

"*Found* her?"

"Yeah."

"Like at the mall or something?"

"I couldn't tell you. One day she wasn't there. The next day there was this little baby and Mom said she was my new sister."

"That's unbelievable." Jack didn't know what else to say. Would *he* ask her about being adopted if he ever saw her again? Probably not.

"It's just something I thought maybe you should know. Probably doesn't make any difference but I guess it's best not to leave anything unsaid, huh?" Jack was going to agree with him but was stopped before beginning when Sam said, "I think you can pull over any time now and we should be able to find it. 'When Two Worlds Collide,'" Sam mused. "I never knew she called it that. That's a cool name for it, I guess."

"Maybe it's even appropriate," Jack said, easing the car over to the side of the road. He didn't have to bother turning off the ignition. It shuddered violently, hissed, and threw up a column of white steam before the engine stopped completely.

He opened his door and stepped out. Sam came out through his side, presumably so he wouldn't have to cut the duct tape away. With Sam's size and girth, the struggle would have been comical under any other circumstances. Standing there, Jack felt like they were an unlikely pair of heroes, if heroes were what they were to become. Jack was short, nearly anemic in his build. He held his cell phone like a weapon. Sam was nearly a foot taller than Jack and easily outweighed him by a hundred pounds. He held the large knife in his right hand. The roll of duct tape encircled his left wrist like a bracelet containing special powers. What kind of special powers? Jack wondered. Adhesiveness? Sam was covered in blood that had now gone kind of crusty brown. Jack thought he looked more like an escaped mental patient.

A meadow spread out before them, its grass yellowed.

He didn't feel nearly as cold as he had earlier, out trudging through the rain. It was like the weather had changed completely. The sun, although dying, peeked through the clouds. The air was much warmer and, because of the rains earlier, felt steamy. The beginnings of a thin ground fog covered the meadow.

At the back of the meadow, merely dark shapes on the horizon for now, were the two train engines, one with a cargo car still attached.

It hit Jack for the first time how extremely odd those trains were.

TWENTY-ONE

"It's so quiet out here," Jack said. The road they had just pulled to the side of was a very narrow one. No yellow lines down the middle. No white lines on the sides. This was where the city saved their money. Not enough people traveled on this road to warrant the upkeep.

"Do you think someone owns all this?" Jack asked.

"Never really gave it much thought. I'm sure somebody somewhere owns it. I don't think there's any bit of property that *isn't* owned these days, is there?"

"I think you're probably right about that."

"I guess we'd better get started, huh?"

Jack patted the cell phone in his pocket to make sure it was there. "Yeah, and we'd probably better hurry. This might not be the place. We don't want to waste all of our time here if it isn't. And, listen, Sam . . ."

"I'm listenin'."

"Whatever happens, we have to stick together. Okay? No losing each other. No getting separated."

"Didn't plan on it. I don't really want to be alone out in the Wilds after dark. Those are some creepy ass woods."

"Let's go then."

They set off across the meadow. It was probably around 200 yards across and maybe that deep as well. Woods were on either side of it and Jack thought it looked like the Wilds were encroaching, threatening to gobble up the meadow and maybe even, eventually, the road.

They cut through the tall grass. It would have soaked their shoes and their jeans if they weren't soaked already. He had now spent the greater part of the day outdoors and knew this was not the greatest type of day to do that. Although it was better now. Now being outside wasn't that bad. It wasn't rainy or cold. It was almost balmy. For this time of year, it was a very rare type of day.

He kept his eyes set on the engines in the distance, watching them get larger and larger.

"So," Jack asked. "You said you've been in those trains?"

"Oh, yeah, I think just about anybody who's ever been a teenager in Alton has been in there. You said you've been there, right?"

"Yeah. Did you ever cross through them? You know, like get to the Wilds by going through the trains?"

"Oh, definitely. It was a, um, natural progression I guess you'd say. That's how we discovered the motel. *The Hotel Eternity*!" He blurted nearly triumphantly. "That's what that old place is called. The Hotel Eternity. It's an awful fancy name for a place that isn't really that fancy at all, if you ask me. It's like when they call bars things like 'Partners' and 'Champs' or 'Winners' . . . You know, like the complete opposite of what you'd find inside. I guess 'Hotel Eternity' is supposed to sound romantic but it's the kind of place you'd go if you wanted to snort cocaine off a hooker's back while you rammed her from behind. Anyway, yeah, I've definitely been through those trains. Why?"

"When I was talking to Tim Fox, he said Gina was afraid to go through the train. She would get in the train on the one side, you know, this side, but then she was afraid to go out the other side of the car. She said that if she stepped off she would be in like . . . another world or something. I guess that's why she thought of calling it 'When Two Worlds Collide.' Now, if she mentioned the name of the place to me, it's possible I forgot, but I *know* she never mentioned that crazy theory."

"You don't think she was serious, do you?"

"I didn't see how she could be and I kind of asked Tim about that too and he said that she was most definitely deathly afraid of getting off on the other side. He never saw her do it. He would even do it himself just to let her know that nothing would happen."

"I guess our Gina could be a little crazy at times."

"But that's completely irrational."

"Unless she knows something we don't know."

That last sentence just kind of hung there in the air, neither of them really expounding on it. Like two drunks who, after having stumbled upon some truth have to look in their beer glasses, silently, to contemplate that truth.

"So," Jack said after a while. "You really think it's possible?"

"Wouldn't you say just about anything is possible at this point?"

"Probably so."

Then, after walking a few more steps, he said, "It's the marks."

"Huh?" Sam said, lost in his own reverie.

"It's the marks."

"Oh," Sam said, inspecting his bandaged left arm. "What do you mean?"

"Well, I wouldn't have thought that anything was possible if it hadn't been for the marks. Until then, I just thought I was an extremely unfortunate fellow. But the marks make me think maybe something else is going on."

"Like something mystical?" Sam asked.

"Maybe," Jack said.

The trains grew even closer. Less than fifty yards away now. He decided to consider the oddity of the situation. He had heard of trains derailing before. Usually due to some kind of mechanical failure. But two engines plowing into each other? It seemed ludicrous. Impossible. Didn't they have extensive safeguards against such a thing? Were tracks even two-way? He didn't know. It seemed like there would be only one way per track but he supposed they *could* go both ways. He didn't really see why not. But then what about schedules? That seemed like one of the most obvious associations with trains. Train schedules. Trains running on time. If scheduling and time were so inherent to locomotion then how could two trains just plow into each other like that?

Unless one had simply come from nowhere.

The thought sent a shiver down his spine. It was that kind of thinking that threatened to drag his mind off into tangents he didn't really want it to go. But the more he thought about it, the more things seemed to be leaning toward the supernatural. Maybe even the mystical, as Sam had put it.

The trains and the brands.

Of course, the trains had been here for as long as anyone could remember. He would have to look up their history if he made it out of this alive. Again, there was an insane thought. Making it out of things alive. That just seemed to be so much more dramatic than what he was used to.

The brands, however, the brands were something new.

He still had Sam's in his jeans pocket.

Now nearly to the trains, he had a thought and frantically pulled the brand out of his pocket, spreading it out in his palm.

"What is it?" Sam asked.

"The brands," Jack began. "The marks. From the very first one, I noticed there was some kind of pattern to them and I think, if you're right about that old hotel, I might have figured them out."

"Explain, please," Sam said.

Transferring the brand to his left hand, he pointed his right index finger along first the left vertical line. Then the horizontal line in the middle. Then the right vertical line.

"See," he said. "That's an 'H'."

Then he ran his finger again along the left vertical line. Then the topmost horizontal line. The second one down, in the middle. The bottom one.

"And that. That's an 'E'. See how they're thicker there?"

A strange expression crossed Sam's face. Maybe it was concern. Maybe it was pity.

"You don't think I'm right, do you?" Jack asked.

"I want to think you're right," Sam said. "I just don't want you to get your hopes up. I mean, we could be way off the mark here. That motel might not even be there, for all I know. It's probably been ten years since I've seen it and the city likes to tear things down that could possibly harbor squatters and bums. I would be more surprised if it were still standing at all."

Jack thought about the mental image in his head from when Mr. Grin had called. It fit. It fit the image of an abandoned hotel perfectly. That would explain why all the furnishings were more wildly out of date than hotel furnishings normally are.

"Yeah," Jack said. "You're right. We'll just have to play it by ear."

The trains were in front of them, reeking of oil and exhaust, even after all these years. They loomed there, larger than life.

"All aboard," Sam said, and slowly climbed up into the freight car.

"Wait!" Jack shouted. A bad feeling soured his stomach.

It was Sam's alarm at Jack's warning that probably got him hurt.

He turned to face Jack and a gunshot rang out. The hand holding the rusty rail disintegrated and Sam tumbled to the ground at Jack's feet. Jack didn't know whether to help him or run.

"Move away," Jack heard from the freight car. It was a voice he recognized all too well. One he'd had to listen to rambling on at unholy lengths about subjects he had no interest in.

Mr. Moran, Dick, stood at the lip of the freight car, a double-barrel shotgun in his hand.

Jack stood in front of the sprawled Sam, holding his stump of a hand against his chest.

"I only got one more shell in this and it ain't intended for you," Mr. Moran said.

"Why are you doing this, Dick?" Jack asked.

But he knew he wasn't really talking to his neighbor. He was talking to whatever that brand had made him. In a sense, by his mere contact, what *Jack* had made him. Snapshots of the other people he had come in contact with that day lightning-flashed through his mind. Quick. Joey at the cafe. There had been a woman in front of him when he got there. How far did this go? Would they be branded as well? What about that woman at the gas station? Jack couldn't remember her name but he remembered all those blue stars under her name. Those blue stars meant she was good at what she did. Would she be good at killing Jack too? Where did it end? There was that old lady on the bus. The one who had crossed herself. And what about the bus driver and the other people on the bus? What about people who had . . . Jesus, what about people who had maybe just seen him from the windows of their homes or the windows of their cars? What about them?

"I'm not moving," he told Mr. Moran.

"You weren't supposed to have no help. Them's the rules."

"How the fuck would you know what the rules are?"

"I know everything he knows."

"Who is he?"

"Well, I think you call him Mr. Grin, don't you?" Mr. Moran laughed a strange toothless laugh. Jack realized he had never seen him laugh before. He had seen him smile plenty of times but he had never seen him laugh and it was a sphincter-tightening thing to witness.

"How could you possibly know that?"

"See, I kinda know everything you know too."

"Put the gun down, Dick."

"Who said you could call me Dick," Mr. Moran said.

Then he pulled the trigger.

TWENTY-TWO

Jack felt the black pall of death fall around him, sure he was shot.

The stinging in his leg took his mind off that.

He had only taken some of the buckshot, biting into the outside of his left leg.

Another second and he realized what happened. Horrified, he turned and looked down at Sam.

Only it wasn't like looking at Sam at all. Most of his head was gone, turned into a red-gray pulp. He dropped down to his knees, between Sam's legs, his back to him, and threw up.

He couldn't remember the last time he had eaten anything. He figured it was mostly coffee, black and burning, clinging to his tongue and his lips.

And it hit him again how very serious this whole thing was. Although he had begun to realize it was a very serious thing a long time ago, there was a gradual escalation to the seriousness of it all. A gradual escalation culminating here.

He looked up at Mr. Moran, Dick, a cold kind of belief freezing his insides.

Dick stood just inside the freight car. Looking at him, Jack knew Dick Moran was nowhere inside of that man. He was back at his house. Back where he had been branded. Part of Jack wanted to kill the man who stood before him. But he knew that would be wrong. It was not this man who had killed Sam. It was not this man who had stolen Gina away from him. It was somebody else. A greater power. Maybe just another man or maybe someone or something far more equipped than anyone Jack had ever known.

"You shot Sam," Jack muttered, in shock, not knowing what else to say.

"I told ya," Mr. Moran said. "Them's the rules. Them's the rules and if you don't follow 'em then I have to make sure you do follow 'em."

Jack stood up, wiping the stinking puke from his chin. He had to get away from here. He had to get through the car Mr. Moran was blocking and to the hotel. He was convinced Gina would be in the hotel. She had to be. Or else it wasn't a game at all, was it? If there wasn't any sort of ending, if there wasn't any clear-cut winner, then it was more like a trick than a game.

When Jack reached the ground just in front of the car, Mr. Moran transferred the barrel of the gun to his hands and swung it out in a giant loop. Normally, if this were the actual Dick Moran, Jack wouldn't have been frightened of that swinging stock. There wouldn't have been any real muscle power behind it. But this was the branded Dick Moran. This was undoubtedly a Dick Moran of near superhuman strength.

He waited until the gun completed its arc before rushing the car and grabbing Mr. Moran around his skinny old man ankles.

He tried to drive the stock of the gun down into Jack's head but Jack quickly yanked his ankles and sent him sprawling back into the car. Quickly, Jack heaved himself inside and pounced on Moran.

The gun had come loose in his fall and lay in a far corner of the car, out of reach.

He rested his ass on Mr. Moran's scrawny chest and put his knees on his upper arms.

Mr. Moran stared at him, an expression of fury twisting his face, and tried to lift Jack off. Jack had no doubt he could be bucked off if Mr. Moran fully caught his bearings.

Yanking Mr. Moran's shirt sleeve up, Jack bared the brand on his left forearm. Now, looking at it, even momentarily, he didn't see how it could be anything but an 'H' and an 'E'.

He pinched Mr. Moran's papery skin between his thumb and

forefinger and gave a healthy yank. Jack put the brand in his pocket.

The old man screamed, spitting at Jack.

Then he was calm, lying there on the floor of the car and breathing deeply.

Jack knew the decent thing would be to stick around at least long enough to ask him if he was okay but he was through doing the decent thing. At least for the day.

Sam was dead but he couldn't mourn.

Mr. Moran may be injured, may even need medical attention, but he couldn't wait to find out.

Gina was the only thing that mattered.

And now, if he didn't find her, then Sam's blood was on his hands. Sam's death would have been in vain. Jack wasn't going to let that happen. He was going to do what he started out to do and now, he had no doubts, he would relish the kill. If he could find Mr. Grin, there would be no hesitation. No conscience. No mercy.

Jack took a deep breath and plunged off the other side of the freight car and there was something inside him that hoped Gina was right. Because he thought, maybe, in a magical world, the odds would be a little more even.

TWENTY-THREE

Jack stepped out of the freight car and into the Wilds. This was the most thickly wooded area in Alton, the rest of it, like most mid-size cities, given up to overdevelopment and urban sprawl. The trees, still with most of their leaves, made it seem prematurely dark. Full dark was still a couple hours away but, in the Wilds, dusk was upon him. Still thinking about the others who may be branded—Joey, the customer in the coffee shop, the bus driver, the old lady on the bus (hell, maybe *everyone* on the bus), the cashier at the gas station—made him nervous. Here, in the Wilds, there were plenty of places for them to hide.

He stood for a moment, hesitant to move. Whichever direction he chose, he knew, might be his last. He may not have the chance to go back and repeat his steps or choose some other path.

Time was short.

His phone vibrated in his pocket.

The now familiar dual sensation of hope and dread made its way down his spine to sit in the pit of his stomach.

He pulled the phone from his pocket, wondering exactly when he had put it back in there, and flipped it open.

"Yeah."

"JACK! JACK!" Gina's voice. Frantic. Frantic but welcome. She was still alive. She was still able to scream and that was something. That was everything to him, at this point.

"Gina. Gina."

"He knows where you're at. He's coming after you—"

And her voice was gone. Replaced with grunts and moans. The sounds of smacking flesh. Screams. Screams unlike Jack had ever heard before.

But where are you, Gina? he thought. Where the hell are *you*?

"She's right, shit crawler."

Then the connection was gone.

A shot cracked through the early dusk.

Jack's stomach lit up, on fire. He'd been hit.

He dropped to his knees, his head jerking in the direction of the shot, wondering when the next one was going to come. He was not going to let it end this way. He told himself it couldn't end this way. He couldn't even begin to wrap his mind around it at this point. To wake up to a beautiful Sunday morning only to die in the woods beside some abandoned trains was not something he could understand.

Another shot followed but that one must have missed because he didn't feel any biting pains.

Then he saw her.

Moving behind a tree less than twenty feet away.

The woman from the gas station.

It was like everything he had thought was coming true. He felt helpless but knew he couldn't just lie down and die. He felt helpless because he wondered who else could be surrounding him. And he wondered how they had guns. Well, he thought, Mr. Moran was kind of a given. Old Republican shits like him always had guns. And, of course, he thought, the woman from the gas station probably kept a gun under the counter or in the safe. For self-defense.

While she was behind the tree, he darted up, off to his left, and hid himself behind a tree. What a fun game this is, he thought.

She started out from behind her tree and momentarily stopped when she noticed Jack was no longer on the ground where she had left him.

Desperately, he scanned the ground around him for anything he could use as a weapon. He also scanned the surrounding woods to see if there was anyone else lurking there.

Nothing.

On both accounts. Nothing.

The only thing he could do was try and work himself behind the mad woman. She walked toward the freight car and Jack crept to the next tree. If he knew where he was going he would simply take off in that direction but he didn't and, with the mad woman, the branded woman, wandering around, he didn't have the time to stand around and try to decide.

The pain in his stomach eliminated whatever patience he may have had left. Luckily, the wound didn't seem to be an incredibly huge one and he figured it must have missed most of his vital organs.

The woman continued to stand there, hunched over. Jack realized she was searching for some kind of scent. Trying to pick him up.

His time was short. And, he thought, he could really use her gun. She had already fired two shots and that meant there were probably at least four more in there. If there were going to be other people in these woods hunting him, those four shots would be essential.

He had to try and take her down before she could manage to get any more off.

Taking a deep breath, trying to ignore the searing pain in his gut, he darted out from the tree, rapidly approaching the woman.

Drawing closer, he realized how burly she was. Taking her down might not be as easy as he thought. Nearly to her, he tripped over a branch and went flying. Luckily, he hit her in the back of the knees before she could even turn around.

She went down and he was immediately upon her, trying to seize her gun before she could aim it at him.

Her lips pulled back in an angry snarl. He saw the brand, burned into her left forearm.

She fired off another shot but it went astray. Reflexes, he thought.

She tried to throw him from her but he held on, digging his knees into her solar plexus. He put his left hand around her thick left wrist, his fingertips sinking into the soft flesh. With his right hand, he grabbed the lump of flesh bearing the brand. All the while, she pounded on his back with her right hand. Each blow sent shuddering waves of pain and nausea through him.

He tore at the flesh. It came away in his hand and he now held another brand like some bizarre trophy. Up this close to her, he could read her nametag, the one with all the little smiley faces. Her name was Donna. He remembered now. Donna was lucky, he thought. Donna almost died. But as soon as the brand was yanked from her flesh, Donna just lay there like she had been somehow . . . *deactivated* was the only word Jack could think of to describe it.

She didn't cry out in pain.

She didn't thrash.

Clearly, she no longer wanted to kill him.

She just lay there, that far-away look in her eyes. Jack grabbed the gun, keeping her from seeing it.

"You look familiar," she said, dreamily.

"You waited on me earlier. At the gas station," he said.

"Where am I?" she asked.

"You're out by the train tracks. You need to go home and get something on your arm before it gets infected."

She nodded without really understanding what he said. He grabbed her arm and held it up in front of her. Her eyes widened. "Ohhh," she said. "How'd that happen?"

"Must have fallen. Lucky I found you out here," he said.

He got up from her before she could wonder about why he was straddling her.

"I gotta go," Jack said.

He began backing away from her, still scanning all around the woods.

Gina had said Mr. Grin would be coming after him but did that mean the man himself would seek him out or did it mean he would be sending the branded after him?

Donna stood up, still dazed, and began drifting back to the freight car. He figured she would make it home eventually. Looking down at the twisted piece of skin in his hand, he realized he didn't need another one and dropped it on the ground. Then he stopped, bent down, and picked it back up. He didn't know why. Routine, he supposed. He stuck it in his right pants pocket with the other brands.

TWENTY-FOUR

Dusk deepened into night. He continued to wander, lost, through the Wilds.

How big were they? he wondered. How long did they go on?

Things were not right, had not been right for a very long time, and it was easy for him to imagine the Wilds continuing forever. From now until his death. He refused to see that his death was something inevitable, trying to ignore the pain from the buckshot in his legs and the bullet in his stomach. He felt around on his back to see if he could feel an exit wound but he didn't. He imagined the bullet sitting in there. At times, he thought he could even feel it. He coughed and spat mucous into his hand, checking for blood. He'd always thought that was serious, when blood came from areas it normally shouldn't.

The air was cooling down again. A mist swirled through the woods. They were impossibly dark. No streetlights or lights from passing cars. No warm glows from the windows of houses. He missed the light. He searched desperately for the light, any light, keeping his ears open for sound. At this point, he thoroughly expected to be attacked by just about anyone. Nothing was outside his sphere of paranoia. Luckily, he had Donna's gun. Jack didn't know guns but he figured it was a .22 revolver. Since he had been hit by one of its bullets, he hoped it was only a .22. Those, he thought, were the least lethal. Checking the cylinder, he saw that it did indeed have three bullets left. It was amazing he even knew how to do this.

Sometimes watching movies paid off.

Time was running out. He would not hesitate shooting anyone. He probably wouldn't hit them if he shot at them anyway. As long as he didn't hit them in the heart or the brain they probably wouldn't die. Just look at *him*. He was limping along just fine after taking a shot.

He pulled his phone out to check it and noticed it was now dead.

His heart sank, but a part of him was grateful the battery had lasted this long. It was nearly dead this morning. Jack was woefully neglectful about charging it. But that meant all contact was severed until he found Mr. Grin and Gina.

Or until Mr. Grin found him.

He thought again about Mr. Grin coming for him. That made a strange sort of sense. If Mr. Grin could catch him before he made it to Gina, even if Jack managed to take him out, there was no guarantee he would find Gina. If she were even still alive.

He didn't want to think about that but he had to. He was dealing with a complete and total psycho. Not just any complete and total psycho, either. One who was gifted with something like supernatural powers. To think Mr. Grin would even come close to losing this battle was something Jack didn't think was possible.

His mind felt fevered.

His stomach burned.

His legs were rubber. He felt like he could collapse at any minute.

But up ahead . . .

Yes, up ahead, he could see a light. Something that could very easily be a sign for a motel. Only, if it was abandoned, why would its sign still light up?

Behind him, he heard shuffling noises.

He turned around to look in that direction and, in the wan moonlight, he saw them.

All of them.

Everyone he thought might become branded. They were all right there behind him. Joey. The woman in front of him at the cafe. The bus driver. The old lady on the bus. Amber, Tim's teen bimbo. And, of course, Tim himself.

Jack aimed the gun at them.

What would it help?

He was outnumbered. If he actually managed to hit any of them, which he highly doubted he could, one of them would still be on him.

He didn't have time to think.

He didn't have time to stand here and take them on individually or as a group. He had no particular desire to hurt any of them.

So he ran.

He ran toward the light he thought he had seen.

His legs protested but they moved. His stomach burned and twisted in pain. Running, he imagined the bullet in there, jostling all around, a little metal virus. His lungs groped for air and, all the while, he could hear that mob behind him, coming closer and closer.

The Wilds began to clear a little bit and Jack could see the light ahead of him was coming from what *had* to be the motel. It didn't come from the sign like he had originally thought. It looked like it came from the lobby. As he sped closer, he could see there *was* a sign, standing in the middle of the parking lot, but it was not lighted, although it looked like it had been at one time. The letters were blackened. The whole sign looked like it was covered in soot. It announced itself, in a font no longer used on signs, as the Hotel Eternity.

Jack's feet smacked the asphalt as the bus driver opened fire. He saw sparks from the corner of his eye. Waited for the bite of another shot. Felt the cool, slightly slimy steel of the lobby door's handle. Pulled the door open. And stepped into another world.

TWENTY-FIVE

The lobby was cool and brightly lit. Jack half-expected the mob following him to come charging through the door or shoot until the glass shattered.

He wondered how the door still had any glass in it at all. The windows were the first thing to go on any abandoned building. Especially one out in the middle of nowhere that had been abandoned for as long as this place.

He could see them out there, standing around in a lame half-circle, looking at one another. They grunted and snarled and, for a horrifying moment, Jack thought they were going to rip each *other* apart. And found himself wanting exactly that to happen. If they did that it meant he didn't have to deal with them anymore.

But they didn't.

The bus driver pushed his hat back on his head and reached out with his right hand to touch the brand on the cafe lady's arm. Then he pulled it off. She did the same for him. Joey pulled off the old lady's brand and she returned the favor. Tim Fox and Amber removed each other's brands, like some sadomasochistic form of foreplay.

All of them holding a disgusting tab of skin in their fingertips, they approached the door of the lobby and placed the brands on the cement in front of it. Then they drifted back toward the Wilds.

Jack stood there, sick and sweaty, marveling at what had just happened.

He fought the urge to vomit or pass out.

"May I help you?" a voice said from behind him. Jack knew from the voice that it wasn't Mr. Grin.

He turned and a man stood behind the counter in the lobby.

Looking around the lobby, Jack thought the Hotel Eternity did not look abandoned at all. A little outdated maybe but it looked like a finely restored vintage room rather than some abandoned place. He was not at all surprised to find something he had not expected.

Jack approached the counter.

"I'm trying to find Gina," he said. "Do you know where she is?"

The clerk was a thin man, wearing a dark red shirt and brown tie. His hair was close-cropped, his eyes a hypnotic blue. The corner of his mouth twitched in a feeble attempt at a smile.

"Do you have something for me?" the clerk said. He had a name tag and Jack read, half-amused, the name 'Mr. Thick'.

"What do you mean . . . like money?"

"Something like that."

"I don't have any money. And I don't have time to play games. Look . . . I'm in a very serious situation here . . . Maybe you can help me out, huh? Do you have anyone staying here?"

"More people than we can count."

"Have you seen anyone come through here who looks like, I don't know, a portly guy who smiles a lot?"

"I can't help you without some form of offering."

Mr. Thick's upper lip again twitched slightly, as though he was trying to stifle a laugh and Jack thought he saw a faint . . . *flicker* run through the man. Like a line going down the TV when the cable's getting ready to go out.

Jack pulled out his cell phone and put it on the counter. Mr. Thick quickly slapped it away, sending it thumping onto the floor.

"Vulgar things," he said, smoothing the front of his fitted shirt.

"I'm sorry," Jack said. "That's all I have."

"Then I cannot help you."

Mr. Thick turned and Jack saw another one of those strange ripples course over his body.

"Wait!" Jack said. He reached into his other pocket and pulled out the three brands, laying them out on the counter.

Mr. Thick looked down his long nose at the hunks of bloody, some hairy, flesh.

"That is not nearly enough," he said.

"Hold on," Jack said.

He crossed the lobby to the front door. Opening the door, he bent down, his stomach screaming, and picked up the six brands placed there.

"How 'bout now?" he said, putting those on the counter.

"I may be able to help you."

"Great," Jack said.

"But you'll have to help me get this laundry to the back."

"Sure. Whatever."

Mr. Thick ducked down behind the counter and came back up. "I can't lift it by myself," he said.

Jack went around behind the counter, looking down at the huge white canvas laundry bag.

"Where you going with it?" he asked.

"Just to the back room there."

"I'm not in the best condition right now."

"I don't really need your brawn. It's just . . . awkward is all."

Together they bent down and hoisted up the heavy laundry bag. Jack thought his insides were going to squeeze out through the bullet wound but the fact this man may be able to help him eased the pain somewhat. They carried the laundry bag through a door and into a room containing a heavy mahogany desk and some gray filing cabinets and not much of anything else.

"On the desk is fine," Mr. Thick said.

With a final heave, they placed the bag on the desk.

Mr. Thick smoothed his greasy, thinning hair back onto his scalp and said, "Guests really shouldn't be in the office."

Jack stared at him. Mr. Thick stared back. Apparently he wasn't going to move until Jack went back to the other side of the counter. Jack crossed back over to the other side of the counter, leaning against it for support. Mr. Thick came out of the office and cast a suspicious, sweeping glance around it before shutting the door and turning back to Jack. He again smoothed his shirt, at least as out-dated as this lobby. He cleared his throat and said:

"The man you're looking for is not who you think he is. He smiles because he's out of his skin. Try looking in the Utility Shed."

And then Mr. Thick was gone. As though he had never been there to begin with. Jack looked down at the counter, expecting to see that Mr. Thick had taken the brands, and saw nine keys instead. Keys for the rooms, of course, Jack thought.

He felt closer to Gina than he had since staring at her underwear-clad bottom that morning.

He gathered up the keys and put them in his pockets.

TWENTY-SIX

He stepped out into the cold night under a sky the color of old milk.

He had keys.

He didn't know exactly what that meant but the keys were hope. Keys opened doors and Gina might just be behind one of those doors.

He wondered if the motel only had nine rooms or if he would have to be selective about the rooms he entered. But it would all be meaningless if the keys didn't open the door housing Gina, wouldn't it? And there was still the possibility she wasn't here at all. That this was still some part of Mr. Grin's disturbing game. But he didn't want to believe that. Despite the incessant moaning of his body, things felt different. They felt better. They had felt better ever since those people had removed their brands and placed them in front of the door. In a way, he felt like that was their way of telling him he had made it. Because they had been sent here to stop him and if they were just giving up then that meant there wasn't anything to stop, right?

It made sense to Jack.

But again, he wondered if the brands were the work of Mr. Grin or somebody else. In the end, he figured, they had helped him so maybe they weren't Mr. Grin's. Of course, if all they did was get him closer to Mr. Grin and, therefore, death, then he supposed that probably wasn't a lot of help.

The keys were in his left pants pocket. He went to the first door and tried each key. Once a key didn't work, he placed it in his back pocket. None of the keys opened the first door.

He went to room number two and began trying the keys. The third key opened the lock. Pulling the pistol from the back of his pants, he opened the door just a crack, listening. If Mr. Grin was in there, he assumed he would probably pounce on him as soon as he stepped into the room.

He heard nothing. Slowly, he eased himself into the room.

It was disorienting.

The room was not at all what he expected.

It wasn't really a hotel room at all. And it was very loud, filled with the cacophonous sound of furious typing and the flapping wings of birds.

The room was huge. It reminded him of a warehouse or a large barn. It was full of people, busy at desks. The room was very brightly lit, which he found odd because he hadn't seen the glow of a light from outside. The enormous room's roof was crisscrossed with a number of wooden beams. Roosting on these beams were thousands of nondescript birds. Probably pigeons or sparrows, he thought. He didn't really know birds. A giant ladder was propped against one of the beams.

A squat man with a toupee approached him.

"You gonna get to work?" he asked.

"I . . ." Jack didn't really know how to begin. "I don't think I work here."

"Ah, anybody can work here. It's easy as pie. Just watch that guy."

He watched a slender man in a suit and tie and rectangular black-framed glasses stand up from a desk and cross the wooden floor to the ladder. Quickly, expertly, he climbed the ladder. He slowed once he got closer to the top of the ladder, moving stealthily, cautiously. After reaching the staggering height of the beam, he reached out, slowly, and then, lightning-quick, grabbed onto one of the birds.

The squat man in the toupee grunted. "He got 'im a good un."

The man in the suit, tucking the bird into his blazer, descended the ladder in a hurry. He crossed back to his desk where a computer monitor and keyboard rested. The monitor was the old clunky kind.

The man opened the top of the monitor and placed the bird inside. Jack noticed there was a crank on the right-hand side of the monitor. The man cranked the crank and a bluish glow came from the monitor.

"He'll have to work all night on that," the squat man said.

Jack didn't know why he was here. "I think I have the wrong room," he said. "I'm sorry."

"The damn hotel's like that. Took me forever to find this place. I still haven't found my way out. None of us has. If you ever need a job, you come back. There's plenty of birds. And plenty of light."

He slid his gun back into the waistband of his jeans, realizing he wasn't in any sort of danger, and cautiously attempted to slink out of the room.

"Before you go," the squat man said, gesturing down at Jack's gut wound. "You should go to Room 12. Might be able to help you with that."

"Thank you," Jack said. "Thanks a lot."

He wondered if he should go directly to Room 12 or try all the other doors between here and there. He decided to try all the other doors. If he did run into Mr. Grin before he made it to Room 12, he didn't see how this little gunshot wound was really going to hurt his chances.

He had eight keys left. How many more rooms were there?

He thought about what the clerk had said to him. *The man you're looking for is not who you think he is. He smiles because he's out of his skin. Try looking in the Utility Shed.*

Yes. He would have to do that. He would have to remember a utility shed. Suddenly, he wasn't so sure he could remember anything. He let the clerk's three somewhat bizarre, not really connected sentences replay in his mind because, of all the things to hold onto, he thought maybe that was it. He wasn't even sure if he could remember what he saw in the last room. It didn't seem to make a lot of sense. It was more like a dream. He felt that it was likely he was still lying back in the Wilds somewhere, passed out from pain or maybe even dying.

None of the keys opened Room 3.

Onto Room 4.

Again, none of the keys worked.

Room 5 opened on the first key and again, he underwent the same ritual of first cracking the door and listening for sound. Nothing. He slid the gun from his waistband.

This room was darkened.

He felt along the wall for a switch and, finding it, flipped it up. Once the room was lighted, he felt a staggering sense of déjà vu. This was the room he had seen in his mind when Mr. Grin had called the one time . . . The time he forced Gina to give him head at gunpoint. Maybe all the rooms were the same or maybe, he thought, maybe this *was* the room.

The bed was mussed and he thought, if he breathed deep enough, he could smell Gina's exotic scent along with a more primal, desperate stench that maybe accompanied all hotel rooms. The smells of smoke and semen and sweat.

Over the headboard of the bed was a small smear of blood. Probably made by a hand. He thought of Gina bracing herself against the wall while Mr. Grin plowed her from behind. A blinding fury shot through his brain. His stomach lurched in revolt. Collapsing to his knees, he braced himself against the foot of the bed and vomited on the dirty dark green carpet.

Nothing here, he thought.

Seven keys left. Seven keys left and nothing here. The man you're looking for is not who you think he is. He smiles because he's out of his skin. Try looking in the Utility Shed.

The Utility Shed.

The Utility Shed.

Room 12 and maybe someone there could make the pain go away. Who could he really expect to find in a tiny motel like this? Was there a doctor in Room 12, camped out and waiting for him with an impressive array of sterile surgical instruments? He doubted it.

He doubted everything.

He stood up and wiped the puke from his chin, backing out of the room, putting the gun back in the waist of his jeans and not even bothering to shut the door behind him.

What the hell was this place?

A person could go insane here.

All part of the game. It's all part of the game, Jack.

But he didn't want to play the game anymore. He never wanted to play the game to begin with. He just wanted it to be over. He didn't know how much longer he could continue. His whole body was starting to feel like an open, throbbing wound.

"*Gina!*" he screamed, half-expecting her to answer him. "*Gina!*"

Nothing.

Just the silence of an abandoned motel parking lot way on the outskirts of a mid-size city. Looking at it, he saw nothing unusual. Even the light from the lobby was now dimmed. And the door to the lobby looked the way he expected it to look, all shattered dirty glass.

But he was just in there. He was just *in there* and it didn't look that way at all.

Onto Room 6. Room 6. Seven more keys. His mind sang songs of madness. He was losing it. There was absolutely no doubt about that. And if Mr. Grin had come looking for him then why the fuck hadn't he found him yet?

The man you're looking for is not who you think he is. But Jack didn't know who the hell he thought he was other than that vague sense of a smiling fat man.

He now had two keys in his back pocket.

None of the remaining keys opened Room 6.

What if that was the room he needed to be in, though? What if that was the room Gina was in?

He thought about breaking down the door but he doubted his body could take it. No. His body would break before the door would. Stepping back from the door, looking at the door to Room 7, he felt a strange sense of calm.

Things would either work out or they wouldn't.

That was it. After chasing itself all day, that was the only answer, the only *reason* his mind could come up with.

Things would either work out . . . or they wouldn't.

And if they didn't, he supposed there would be little time to think about the consequences.

So far, something had brought him here. He didn't like to think of it as anything divine. It was really more a series of coincidence. And, really, where was 'here' anyway? It could be the place of his potential death. Or it could be the place of Gina's rescue. It was already, most probably, the place of Gina's rape and torture.

Door number seven was a no.

Same with Room 8.

Room 9 opened on the second key.

The room was immaculate. Brightly lit. Clean smelling, even. A non-smoking room? No. They probably hadn't even come up with those by the time the Hotel Eternity went out of business. A piece of paper sat on the bedside table. It was covered in black symbols that looked like stick figures. It begged him to look at it and think about its meaning but he didn't think he had time for that. He folded it up and put it in the breast pocket of his t-shirt because it was something, because it was *anything*.

A third key in the back pocket.

The gun in his waistband.

Six keys left.

Onto Room 10.

Nothing.

Room 11.

Nothing.

Room 12.

This was the room. He didn't think it could have come any sooner. If there was something in this room that could help him, he didn't even care if it was just a painkiller of some sort, he wanted in it.

The fifth key opened it.

Now there were four keys in his back pocket and five in his front. He pulled the gun out. Eased into the room. Felt a further cool sense of calm surround him as he turned on the lights and looked around.

TWENTY-SEVEN

Stepping into the room was like stepping outside.

Maybe he *had* stepped outside. It smelled like outside.

But everything was still *arranged* like it was a motel room. There were several bales of hay, the smaller rectangular kind, the kind people buy around Halloween, in place of a bed. Where a bedside table should have been was a tree. He even thought he saw what very well could have been a bedside table *in* the tree, about halfway up, as though the tree had grown over it, somehow overtaking it. The carpet was a mat of very soft moss. He wanted to take his shoes off so he could feel it on his feet. He probably would have if there weren't more urgent matters at hand. He looked up to see if there was a ceiling but he couldn't tell. If there *was* a ceiling, it was black as the night sky. The room glowed like a full moon night but he couldn't find the source of the light. The walls to his right and his left were lined with high cornstalks, well over seven feet tall. He wondered how far back they went. If he went drifting off into them, would he eventually become lost in some sort of corn maze? The wall in front of him, the one beyond the hay bed, was a meadow. It looked very much like the meadow he and Sam had walked through to get to the train tracks.

The air out there was thick with fireflies. Perhaps these were what provided the light. He didn't see how he could resist going toward them and, he reckoned, he didn't really have any choice.

Things would either work out or they wouldn't.

If something in the distance called to him, beckoned to him, then he felt as if he had an obligation to go toward it. It might be the thing that helped him. And, besides, if he didn't find what he was looking for out there, at least there was a nice open meadow for him to lie down and die in. He took a deep, burning breath, tried to ignore the bullet in his gut, and crossed the room.

Passing the strange hay bed, he reached out his hand and let it brush along the surface as though his sense of touch could reassure him this was real. If this wasn't real, however, his reality had ended some time ago. Touching the stiff hay, he realized he hadn't drawn his gun before entering this room. Was it because of what the squat man with the toupee had said? Had he actually trusted him? If who he was looking for was not who he thought it was then who was to say that the squat man with the toupee wasn't Mr. Grin?

His head hurt. He thought his head hurt almost as much as his stomach. If he didn't find Gina soon, if something didn't happen soon, he thought he might actually die. If he didn't die because of the injuries, then the pain would prevent him from pressing on and he now feared he might be so lost he could never find his way back.

He crossed into the meadow and his strange dreamlike sense intensified even more. The air in the meadow was warm and humid, as if on a summer's night. He saw a small structure in the distance and wondered what it was. He watched the millions of fireflies circle around in the air and come toward him. At first he was frightened of them and then he remembered they were just fireflies, lightning bugs, and couldn't really hurt him.

Within seconds, they covered his entire body.

As if on command, they all stung at the same time.

The pain was immense. It was different than the gunshot pain. It was somehow more . . . clear.

It was sharp and crisp like a needle prick and it sent him to his knees. He felt them crawl in through the gut wound and the buckshot on his leg, under the duct-taped pad and into the stab wound. Felt them twitching around in there, the pain becoming white, blinding.

Then the pain was gone, like that, and the lightning bugs flew back off into the night. They pulled the duct tape off, lifted it into the air, and he thought he could actually see one of them clasping the .22 bullet between its eyelash legs.

He lay there in the meadow, looking up at a black, starless sky, the gun digging into his back, wondering if he would be able to move.

It wasn't just their stinging pain that was gone. It was all the pain.

He put his hand on his left side, just below the ribs, where the bullet had gone in. He fingered the hole in his shirt but felt nothing but smooth, uninterrupted flesh below that. He poked the spot. No pain at all. Amazing. The same with the stab wound. He couldn't believe it. He ran his hand down to his left calf. Again, he felt the tiny holes the buckshot had made in his jeans but the only thing he felt on his leg was hair.

Five keys left.

No pain.

Things were looking good.

He stood up, feeling reborn. He ran toward the structure in the distance, his heart pounding fresh and renewed in his chest. Soon, he was at the structure.

It sat low to the ground, a blocky cinderblock building with a silver corrugated tin roof. It was little more than a shed.

He walked around it until he found an ugly brown door with a shiny stainless-steel knob. Written on the door in runny yellow spray paint were the words "Utility Shed."

He pulled the gun from his pants with his left hand.

The door opened on the third key.

TWENTY-EIGHT

Harsh fluorescent lighting stung his eyes.

He put a hand above his brow and squinted into the room.

John Briggs was there.

John Briggs was the foreman at The Tent. Jack had probably never exchanged more than five words that were not work-related with him on any given day.

He hung upside down. Jack shook his head in confusion, a dreadful realization creeping up on him.

A metal bar ran across the small interior of the Utility Shed. A piece of rope wrapped around Briggs' ankles, hanging him from the bar. He looked like a dead piece of meat. His shirt had slid up his ample stomach. His arms were extended, fingertips mere inches from the cement floor. His thin hair hung from his scalp. And his face muscles were slack, eyes open but staring straight ahead, the corners of his mouth curving toward the floor. Jack didn't see what part he could possibly play in this.

Unless John Briggs was Mr. Grin. Jack moved closer to the suspended body, studying it. Was it possible?

He couldn't think of ever having seen John Briggs smile. In fact, he didn't know if he had ever seen Briggs' mouth, buried, as it usually was, behind the painter's mask. Briggs was all business. There to work. There to make sure others were working. Not a grinning type of person. But he was smiling now. He was smiling because he was hanging upside down.

120

Jack thought about the voice on the phone. It was entirely possible. The more he studied him, the more he was certain John Briggs was Mr. Grin. That's why the voice had sounded vaguely familiar. It was John Briggs but it was a *smiling* John Briggs, someone Jack had never heard before.

Jack contemplated shooting him but he seemed . . . restrained. And unconscious.

Had Gina somehow managed to escape his clutches? Had Gina managed to do this? Jack didn't think it was possible. Briggs had to be close to 300 pounds and he just couldn't see Gina being able to string him up.

It was just too simple.

This couldn't be it. He couldn't just aim the gun and fire it at this hanging thing and think he had caught Gina's captor.

The man you're looking for is not who you think he is. He smiles because he's out of his skin.

That seemed simple to Jack. Mr. Grin was not in John Briggs. If he was looking for Mr. Grin and he now *thought* it was John Briggs that meant it couldn't be John Briggs. What he saw in front of him was a husk. The skin. Whatever was once inside that skin was now out of it. Happily out of it. Smiling because he was out of his skin.

Suddenly, he found himself thinking about the dirt at The Tent. Where *did* that dirt come from? Where did it go? Grisnos? He had been a stellar geography student and didn't recall any country called Grisnos. Could The Tent have anything to do with this? He wondered what he had been doing the past three years. Would Mr. Thick, the strange flickering man at the front counter, know where Grisnos was? Jack thought maybe he would.

He had a revelation. It came upon him in a rush and he didn't have the time to question it. He didn't *want* to question it.

There was something in the dirt. Something. . . otherworldly. It came from one world and went to another. Something in the dirt. Something that made some people sniff it. Something that made some people forget. Something that, over time, rotted people's insides. And it had rotted the insides of John Briggs. Rotted them so much they couldn't stand to be in his body anymore. Maybe he was so rotten inside he didn't have any idea what he was doing. But why Gina? Why Jack?

He put the gun in the back of his pants.

He thought maybe it was time for him to come out of his skin, too.

He reached into his breast pocket and pulled out the piece of paper with the stick figure drawings on it.

Now that he had seen Briggs hanging in front of him, the meaning of those drawings seemed obvious. It was an instruction sheet telling him how to suspend himself like Briggs. He didn't know if it would help. He desperately wanted things to work out. This was one sick mindfuck of a puzzle but he was beginning to understand it for the puzzle it was.

Another rope hung from the metal bar. There was a loop at the end of it. All he had to do was place both feet in the loop, grab the other end of the rope dangling above him, and pull.

He didn't know how he was going to stay up there. He imagined the second he let go of the rope he would just go plummeting headfirst onto the cement. Stepping into the loop, he put the instruction sheet to use.

Once he was upside down, everything fell out of his pockets. All the keys clattered to the floor. The gun hit the floor with a smack and he was thankful it didn't discharge.

Hesitantly, he took his hands away from the rope.

He didn't go plummeting to the floor. He stayed just where he was. He felt his muscles slacken. He felt his mouth open into a grin. He didn't like the feeling at all. Now was not a time to be smiling.

He thought of Gina as he closed his eyes.

He thought of the dirt-smudged picture of Gina he kept in his work area at The Tent. Was it possible Briggs had seen that picture and thought he absolutely had to have Gina? Was it possible everything had spiraled out of control from there? Was it even possible that Gina may have at one time slept with Briggs? Maybe he was one of her scorned lovers and this was his attempt to get back at her. And not just her but the most important person in her life.

Or . . .

Or maybe it went beyond this world. Maybe it went all the way to that other world that smacked into Earth when two worlds collided. Maybe Gina couldn't cross through the freight car because she didn't want to go home. Maybe she had been born in another world. Maybe she was adopted because someone helped her escape. Maybe someone wanted to take her back. Maybe Briggs had something to do with that. Maybe whatever had gotten *inside* Briggs had something to do with that. And if Briggs' body was here but his rotten insides were somewhere else then where was Gina's body? And which part of her was being tortured? Her insides or her real body?

And then there were the brands. The brands were definitely supernatural. The brands were definitely not normal. Something had inflicted those brands on all those people. Something had tried to stop Jack from making it to the Hotel Eternity. But once Jack made it, those brands had turned into keys. And the keys would take him where he needed to go. Was that Jack's first victory? Were the keys his reward?

Maybe Jack was going crazy.

He wondered what time it was.

Then he went out.

TWENTY-NINE

The next thing he remembered, Jack was standing there in the Utility Shed looking at his own upside-down body, feeling that stupid, irremovable grin straining at his lips and cheeks. He didn't like the look of his body under those harsh fluorescent lights, next to Mr. Grin, next to John Briggs. He thought he looked unreal. Waxy. Dead.

He looked down at the ground.

The gun was there and, although all the keys had fallen out of his pockets when he suspended himself, there were now only the four unused keys. He scooped the keys and the gun up. He opened the door of the Utility Shed to the outside, not bothering to close it. What if he closed it and wasn't able to get back in? He didn't know which was the real him. Was it the guy hanging up in the Utility Shed or was it the body he now inhabited. He felt like himself. From what he could see of himself it seemed like this body was just the same as his old body.

What a weird thought. A new body and an old body. But today had been a day of weird thoughts.

Or was yesterday a day of weird thoughts?

He noticed the sun was out over the meadow and felt a wave of fear.

It had to be coming up on the 24-hour mark. How long had he spent in that shed? Was that the wrong thing to do? Had he blown everything?

As quickly as possible, he began walking through the meadow, toward the East, toward the rising sun.

The morning was warm and humid. But he wasn't sweating. Didn't even really feel hot. He felt cool. Detached. He couldn't explain it. He had dropped acid exactly once. He felt a lot like that now. Like he was very much locked inside this new body and he saw everything with some kind of near-geometric clarity, sharper and crisper, hyperfocused. It was so real and so perfect it was dreamlike.

Eventually, he came to the hotel again. It didn't surprise him, even though he had been walking in the opposite direction.

In this light, the hotel looked even more decrepit and run down. Or maybe it was just because he was coming up from behind it. He didn't really remember much about it from before, maybe because it had been dark. There were strange gaps in his memory. He thought about Gina. He thought about Mr. Grin. And he couldn't really seem to think about anything else.

He couldn't remember which door he had opened last. He remembered it was the one he was supposed to open, or so he thought. It was the one the squat man with the hairpiece had told him about. He went around the corner of the hotel. It seemed to be shaped in kind of a blocky horseshoe shape. The first door he came to was, unbelievably, Room 6004.

That couldn't have been right. There was no way this place had over 6000 rooms . . . but questioning was useless. The answers were probably more ridiculous than the questions themselves.

The first key he tried worked. Three more keys. He opened the door onto a perfectly normal-looking room. It was perfectly normal-looking but it didn't really fit the general decor of the other rooms he had seen in the hotel. The walls were all white. He didn't know if he had ever seen a hotel room with white walls. Most things in the room were white. There was a nightstand that was a lighter wood color. That was on the left side of the bed. Over the bed was a large painting or photograph, he couldn't be sure, of a large meadow, more rolling than the one he was just in, with some murderous black clouds. To the right of the bed was a ficus tree.

Hm. It didn't seem like there was anything in this room to see at all.

Then the room started to move.

He felt it pull away from the rest of the motel.

That was when he realized the ficus was not a tree at all. It was a man dressed like a tree. Rather, the tree was kind of attached to his back and the man was completely white. He operated some controls set in the wall. The controls were white also and Jack knew it would have been easy to miss, with them being concealed, as they were, behind the tree.

The disguised man turned to look at Jack and Jack saw that his eyes were completely black. No whites whatsoever and a shiver ran up his spine, tremoring out into his viscera.

"So where are we going?" Jack asked.

The man looked away, back at the controls, and Jack knew he wasn't going to get an answer.

He sat down on the edge of the bed and said, "I really need to find Gina. I don't know if you can help me or not. I'm not even completely sure I'm still alive but, if you know where she is, I would really appreciate you taking me to her. You see, I only have three keys left and I think I'm running out of time. I don't know if I'll even get to use all three keys."

The man turned to look at Jack again, saying nothing. When the man turned his head back around to stare at the wall, Jack saw that the whiteness of the wall had darkened, becoming more like a window.

"Are we on a train?" Jack asked.

The man said nothing.

Now from the window, Jack could see that, indeed, there were tracks spread out before him. He thought about the absurdity of entering a motel room and ending up on a train and then he thought about those two trains serving as something like a gateway to the Wilds and, therefore, the Hotel Eternity itself. Gina had called the train wreck "When Two Worlds Collide." Jack felt the sense of two worlds colliding. He felt it very strongly.

The man, the conductor, turned to look at him again. He couldn't help but think of how creepy the man looked. Painted all white like that and those eyes . . .

The conductor removed his left hand from a lever and held it out to Jack. Jack didn't know what he wanted.

He had three keys left.

He gave one of them to the conductor.

The conductor turned and tried to stick the key into a small hole in front of him. The key didn't fit. He handed the key back to Jack and Jack gave him another key. The conductor fit this key into the hole and turned . . .

Screeching deafened Jack.

He felt the collision, like something immense, engulf his body.

Pain scoured him.

Everything went black.

He screamed himself out and thought about the two keys he now had left.

When he came to he was aware of other screams, not his own and, horrified, realized he had found Gina.

THIRTY

He was in a hotel room. Not surprisingly, it looked a lot like the one he had envisioned. A lot like the one he had seen earlier. Only a lot messier.

He saw Mr. Grin, standing there, grinning.

The next thing he noticed was the smell. It reminded him of a butcher's shop or a hospital. Blood, come, shit, and sex—all the smells crashed into him. Frantically, he scanned the room, knowing he wasn't going to like what he found.

Jack stood on one side of the bed, still reeling from the train ride. Mr. Grin stood on the other. He was covered in blood. Otherwise, he looked the way Jack felt. Somehow different. Like a shiny, newer version of the John Briggs he knew from work. It made him think of a puffy balloon.

"Where is she?" Jack asked.

"She put up a good fight, shit crawler," Mr. Grin said.

"Where is she?"

Mr. Grin reached down to the bed and threw back the covers. Finally, after all the searching, Jack saw Gina.

She was splayed supine on the bed, naked. It looked like she was still breathing but her eyes were closed. She too was covered in blood. Numerous abrasions and bruises were painted across her flesh. Her sex, which she normally kept shaved, looked mutilated. A pool of blood spread around her on the white sheets of the bed.

There were so many questions Jack wanted to ask. So many

questions shooting through his mind. But now was not the time. The questions were all secondary. What he really wanted to do was destroy Mr. Grin.

He came around the bed.

Mr. Grin waited, perhaps eagerly, for him.

Mr. Grin was roughly twice the size of Jack but that didn't stop him. It couldn't stop him. The man had told him on the phone that one of them would have to die. This was the end. One way or the other, this had to be the end. Jack wasn't going to die and he wasn't leaving here without Gina. He wasn't going to let Sam's death be for nothing. He wasn't going to lose everything close to him in one day.

He slid the gun from the waistband of his pants, thankful for this leverage. It didn't look like Mr. Grin had any weapons whatsoever.

Two keys left. A gun in my hand. When he thought that, it all felt so close.

Then he had another thought. *This will make you a murderer.* And he thought that maybe he could have meditated on that. Like maybe he could have found a philosophic way around it. Which Briggs would he be murdering? Which man was the real man? For that matter, which Jack was the real Jack? Was it murder if the other Jack, this Jack, killed someone? He didn't know. Didn't really have any time to think about it. Didn't even know if he really *wanted* to think about it.

"You know you're gonna die, right?" Mr. Grin said.

Jack aimed at Mr. Grin's head, trying to remember how many shells were in the gun. Three, he thought. Three shells and two keys.

The first bullet tore Mr. Grin's left ear off.

Jack wanted to immediately fire the other two bullets at him but then, he thought, that would be it. He might never know the answer to anything. What if Gina died? What if she died before she could tell him anything? What if she didn't *know* anything?

"I know you," Jack said. "Why would you do this?"

Mr. Grin backed up from Jack, held his hand up to his ear and looked down at his bloody palm.

"You'd love to know, wouldn't you?"

"Yeah," Jack said. "I really would like to know why you decided to single-handedly destroy my life."

"Put the gun down."

"What?"

"You heard me, shit crawler. Put the gun down and I'll tell you. We'll have us a little pow-wow."

"How 'bout you tell me and I won't shoot you right away."

"This was supposed to be about two men going at each other hand to hand. Fightin' over a lady. Just like men have did for years."

"I've never fancied myself much of a traditional man."

"Put the fucking gun down or I'll jump on this bed and snap her fucking neck!"

Could Jack live with not knowing any of the answers to this mystery? Would he live at all if he put the gun down?

He didn't know if he would. There was no way he could go hand-to-hand with Briggs. He didn't even really know if Briggs was just a man or if he was something more, something supernatural, capable of inflicting people with brands and forcing them to do his bidding.

Jack faked tossing the gun on the bed and watched Mr. Grin feint toward it. In that split-second he realized the giant man had no intention of telling him anything anyway.

He aimed and fired.

A hole blossomed in the middle of Mr. Grin's forehead.

He took a step back, shook his head, blood flowing freely out of the hole until it collected on the tip of his nose and dripped off.

Jack wished he could quit smiling. This didn't feel like a smiling activity.

"Fucker!" Mr. Grin shouted, now shambling toward him.

The hotel room was small. Jack didn't have anywhere to run or to retreat to. Nervous, he fired off the final shot.

This one caught Mr. Grin in the left eye. It turned to black pulp. Jack kept waiting for him to stop and just drop dead onto the floor because that was what people who had been shot twice in the head were supposed to do, wasn't it? They weren't supposed to just keep coming like there wasn't anything wrong with them at all.

Before he could even think of what to do next, Mr. Grin had him in his grip, stripping the gun from his hand and throwing it onto the carpet.

Mr. Grin threw him easily into the end table. While Jack's previous pains had all been healed, this reassured him he was not immune.

Mr. Grin grabbed a large butcher knife from the bed. The knife's blade and handle were already sticky with blood. Jack hadn't seen the knife until now. If he had seen that before, he would have grabbed it while he still had the gun. Then he would have had *all* the weapons.

Mr. Grin approached him. Bent down over him. Jack smelled the stench like sweaty rotting meat.

He tried to kick him away, feeling helpless, but it was like kicking a stone.

Mr. Grin grabbed the back of Jack's head with his left hand, holding it steady.

"How 'bout we make that grin permanent, shit crawler."

"No," Jack said, trying to force him off.

"I call the shots here," Mr. Grin said.

And he sliced at the left side of Jack's face, opening up his cheek from the corner of his mouth to his ear.

Jack screamed. He didn't want to. Couldn't believe this man had brought him to a scream. He tried to bat the knife out of Mr. Grin's hand but Mr. Grin only brought the haft of it down on his forehead. He felt the crack echo through his body.

Then Mr. Grin opened up the right side of his face.

This was it, Jack thought. He was losing. The pain was already making him waver in and out. He reached around, trying to grab onto something. Trying to grab anything.

Mr. Grin chuckled. "You liked that, didn't ya? Wish the old come farm could see you now but she went out some time ago. Guess the body don't like it when you shove one of these up its ass."

He held the bloody knife up in front of him and Jack didn't have to imagine too hard where all the blood on the bed had come from.

Jack tried to talk but it was very difficult.

"You said you wouldn't hurt her until I got here."

"I don't hear you so well," Mr. Grin chuckled. "Your mouth's all fucked up. Anyways, I guess I got kind of bored."

Mr. Grin stood up and Jack lunged at his knees with everything he had. He felt the man buckle and come down on top of him like a slab of concrete.

The knife entered his back. He heard it punch through the skin, maybe a rib or two, and felt the air whoosh out of him.

Shit, he thought.

A lung. The fucker got a lung.

He felt the knife punch down again and again.

He reached back, trying to grab Mr. Grin's head. And Mr. Grin started biting his arms.

Jack's body feeling like so much meat, he slid out from under him.

He stood up, coughing up a gout of blood.

"No chance, shit crawler," Mr. Grin said.

He, too, was standing. And looked much better than Jack felt.

Jack slid his hand, shaking wildly, into his pocket, palming one of the keys so the point jutted out between his middle and index fingers. It didn't seem like much compared to Mr. Grin's girth and his butcher knife but it was all he had. Behind Mr. Grin, he saw Gina on the bed.

He took a quick step toward Mr. Grin and took a swing. The tip of the key punched into his right eye.

"Fucker!" Mr. Grin shouted, clenching the knife in his fist and driving it into Jack's skull.

He waited for the blackness but it didn't come. The knife must not have penetrated all the way through his skull. Before Mr. Grin could work it out, Jack took a savage uppercut at his chin, feeling the key jab into the flesh. Then he stepped away, the knife still lodged in his skull.

Mr. Grin squealed.

Then he went for Gina. Defenseless Gina, there on the bed. He straddled her, wrapping his giant hands around her delicate throat.

Jack thought about trying to work the knife free but knew he didn't have time.

He repositioned the key, determined to open Mr. Grin up.

He jumped behind him on the bed, running the key along his fat throat.

Mr. Grin was growling, strangling Gina.

Jack could hardly breathe. He took the key across Mr. Grin's throat again and again.

He heard something pop and saw Gina covered in a spray of red, smelled the sick copper scent.

With what last bit of energy he had, he yanked Mr. Grin back off the bed. He felt the knife twanging back and forth in his head. Jack pounced on top of Mr. Grin.

On Mr. Grin's chest, he jabbed his hand in through the open neck wound and squeezed the bundle of veins, arteries, and cartilage there. He felt the beating of a heart. He squeezed until it grew faint. Until Mr. Grin's eyes rolled back in his head and the beating stopped altogether. And, unbelievably, once the heartbeat had ceased, he felt something else. He stuck the key into the man's open throat, poking it around inside until he felt the hole. He inserted the key, twisting it until he felt a barrel turn . . .

And found himself sitting on a bloody carpeted floor, the sounds of his ragged breaths very loud in his ears.

Standing up, barely, dazed and staggering, he crossed to the bed, to Gina.

He pulled her up. She was still out.

"Gina," he said. "Gina?"

He could tell she was alive only by the whistling breath between her lips. Was this the real Gina or the Gina-double? And what was the double anyway? Was it the essence of a person? Was it their soul?

If this was Gina's soul, it wasn't in very good shape.

"Gina, it's over . . ."

"Not," she breathed. "Not over."

THIRTY-ONE

He found it hard to breathe and didn't know how much longer he was going to be able to move. If this was *his* soul, then it was dying.

"No, Gina, it's over. He's gone. For good, I think."

"No. Gotta find my body. My real body. Have to."

Her eyelids were heavy, shutting completely only to open slightly.

Okay, so they had to find her body. Then it stood to reason that maybe he should be reunited with his body also. He knew exactly where his was, supposing it wouldn't be too difficult to make it back to the Utility Shed. And, like a faint glimmer in the back of his brain, he thought maybe he knew where to look for Gina's also but he couldn't quite wrap himself around the idea just yet. Complete loss of consciousness couldn't be that far away.

"Come on," he said, standing up on what felt like a moving floor. "We gotta get up."

He grabbed her hands, just happy to feel her flesh against his even if it was this weird glossy spirit flesh. It was something. It was more than he had had in twenty-four hours which, when faced with the prospect of never touching her again, seemed like an eternity.

The knife twanged back and forth in the top of his head. He wanted to pull it out, not liking the way it felt in there, but he was afraid doing so would release a torrent of blood and that might just be all the blood loss his body could take. With a great jerk, he pulled Gina up and over his shoulder. It felt like spikes were driven into his lungs, massive steel clamps squeezing them tight. Once firmly over his shoulder, his knees threatened to buckle. They couldn't—*he* couldn't—buckle. He had come too far to lose it all now. Now he had to go all the way. Never mind that this whole thing didn't make any more sense to him now than it did when he first came home to find Gina missing.

Had to press on.

He went out through the door and realized he had not had to come through a door to enter this room. For that matter, he didn't know how far away it was from the Utility Shed. He half-expected to step through the door and into an entirely alien landscape.

But, once again, he was in that sprawling field, the Utility Shed in the distance. Curiosity dictated he turn and look at the room he had just come from. It seemed to be one-half of the train engine pair that he had seen at the entrance to the Wilds. Only, this looked even more peculiar because the train was stopped, not on any sort of track, and while the front of it was pulverized looking, there was absolutely no evidence of it having hit anything.

Jack felt like they would have to stop at the Utility Shed first to reclaim his body. A strong body would get them back to the hotel that much faster. The hotel was where they needed to go.

One key left.

He wondered if he would need the key to get back in the Utility Shed. If not, he wondered what that key could possibly be. Was there some other trial awaiting them? The desire to simply get it over with propelled him forward. He swam in and out of consciousness. Black periods where he couldn't even remember putting one foot in front of the other. It took every ounce of concentration he had just to keep from falling over or drowning completely in that inky black sleep that called to him.

The Utility Shed almost jumped in front of him.

Gently, he sat Gina down in front of it, resting her back against the cinderblock walls.

The door was cracked.

He pushed it open.

The sight of Mr. Grin, John Briggs, suspended there was shocking. He had to fight an urge to destroy the body but, he told himself, it wasn't the body that was bad. It was possible that Briggs had even been a decent body before whatever it was that Jack had destroyed moved in.

As Jack drew closer to his own upside-down body, he felt the black wave finally pull him under and when he came to he was looking through the open door upside down. All of his pain was gone except for the feeling of blood swelling his head and the numbing prickles throughout the rest of his limbs. On the floor beneath him were the remaining key and the knife. Hysterically, he thought it was nice to know that he didn't have to wander around with a knife in his skull.

He reached his blood-engorged hand out to clasp it around the knife. Raising himself up, he slashed at the rope holding him suspended, bracing for the nasty spill onto the floor. Mainly, he tried to be careful not to hit his head. After several slashes with the knife the rope finally snapped and he came down with a sickening thump on his shoulder blades. The pain was explosive and alive and he thought that, maybe, he liked it.

Taking several deep breaths, he bent to scoop up the key and hurried out of the Utility Shed to gather Gina, making sure she was still breathing.

The breaths were shallower still but they were still there and he hoped the hotel wasn't that far away.

After a few minutes of moving at a quick trot, he could see the roof of the hotel.

Gradually, it became larger and larger and then he stood in the parking lot, ready to enter the cracked and broken front door of the lobby.

Mr. Thick was nowhere to be found.

The door to the office, Jack noticed, was shut. With Gina still slung over his shoulder, he attempted to open the door. Not surprisingly, it was locked. Digging into his pocket for the key, he realized he was breathing quickly and his hands were shaky. This was it. Maybe they had made it. Maybe they would pull through this, after all. After several attempts, he finally fitted the key into the handle, turned, and pushed the door inward.

The laundry bag sat on the now-decayed desk.

Jack unzipped it and saw Gina curled into a ball inside.

At that moment, the office went up in a blinding flash of white.

THIRTY-TWO

Gina stood before him in the decaying office of the Hotel Eternity.

Jack felt the key in his right hand and looked at it. Only, instead of a key, it was the ring he had bought. He dropped to one knee in front of Gina and said, "Gina Marie Black, will you marry me?"

She smiled. It looked like it took everything she had, but she smiled.

"Of course," she said.

And he slid the ring onto her finger.

It felt like the perfect ending but it wasn't over just yet and Jack knew that.

Gina was still in her underwear and tanktop. Jack looked like he had been dragged through the mud. They held hands and walked out into the Wilds, careful to avoid any main roads on their way back home.

They reached the house near sunset. He was sure some people had seen them but probably just wrote it off as a curiosity. As soon as they got home, they showered. Then they went to bed.

Lying there, Gina on his left, he tried to put his arm around her but she moved away. He just wanted to hold her. Just wanted to feel her solidity in his arms, to know she was real. But she didn't want any of it.

There were also a lot of things he wanted to ask her. He figured she must have the answers to so much of it but, lying there and smelling the exotic scent coming from her, he didn't know if he wanted to know all the answers. He realized he didn't necessarily want to know if she knew she was adopted or if she knew where she really came from or why Mr. Grin wanted her for his or why he wanted to destroy Jack. He figured she probably knew the answers to all those questions and maybe that was the great mystery about her. Maybe all of that was what kept him attracted to her.

He cleared his throat, staring at the ceiling.

"If you could choose to forget everything that happened to you, would you do it?"

"Yes," she said unhesitatingly.

"Before I can help you, I just need to know one thing."

She said nothing.

"What happened to Briggs' soul?"

"It went bad."

"What made it go bad?"

"It was always bad."

"You know what I'm thinking, don't you?"

"Yes."

"And there's no chance your soul will go bad?"

"It is a healing substance. But, if a person is bad, it can only accelerate the rot."

Jack nodded.

"Just do it. And then I never want to talk about any of this again."

Jack did it.

THIRTY-THREE

The next morning, Jack went back to The Tent. The car was in worse shape than usual but someone had at least removed the enormous section of tree from it. This was the second day in a row Mr. Briggs hadn't come in and nobody was really working. A number of people had ascended the dirt pile and were engaged in a vigorous game of King of the Mountain. The lady who worked across from Jack lay in her workspace, dirt smeared all over her face, nearly passed out.

No one noticed him.

No one noticed as he took a wheelbarrow and filled it full of that rich, almost black dirt.

No one noticed as he took the wheelbarrow out to his car and filled the trunk with it.

He thought about all the dirt he breathed while working at The Tent. Even with the painter's mask on, it was still a fair amount. He thought about how hard it was to remember what went on there when he came home. In short, he had had an idea.

When he got home, pulling into the driveway, he made Gina come outside and stand by the car.

"Okay," he said. Then he flipped open the trunk.

She grabbed handfuls of the dirt and began smearing it over herself, huffing some up her nostrils and coughing. Jack thought about doing the same thing but realized he never wanted to forget what he went through. He never wanted to forget what led him up to this point in life. Everything after would be simple by comparison.

Mr. Moran stood in his yard.

Oh, God, please, Jack thought. Don't let him make eye contact.

Moran caught him trying to look away and raised his arm, coming over.

"You know," the old man said. "I had the strangest dream about you."

"Really?" Jack said. "Conversations that start with that never end up very good."

"I don't remember it so well anyway. I'm old and addled. Say, why's she coverin' herself in dirt?"

"Don't ask," Jack said. "She's a weirdo."

"Guess so," Mr. Moran said. But he seemed to be so overcome with the oddity of Gina standing at the car and covering herself with dirt that he turned and walked away. He guessed now he knew what it took to end a conversation with Mr. Moran.

Later, as Jack told Gina about Sam, because he had to, he asked her if the dirt had helped and she said she thought it did. She sounded a little bit more like herself. Saddened at the loss of Sam, of course, but there was a bit of the old Gina there. They decided they would wait a few days and then declare him a missing person, realizing it was sort of incriminating that the police would have documentation of Jack being the last person seen with him. But Jack doubted the cop who had come to Sam's apartment was really a cop at all.

The next day, they went to Sam's apartment, just so they could straighten it and remove anything too incriminating. They didn't want the ghost of Sam to be tainted. Jack opened the door, not at all surprised to find that Sam didn't keep it locked. Gina entered behind him.

From the kitchen, he heard a rustling.

"Go wait in the car," he told Gina.

"I most definitely will not."

"Gina, please, I think there's somebody here."

"I'll just stay behind you."

"Fine. But if it is somebody, I want you to take off running.

"Hello?" Jack called toward the kitchen, wishing he had a gun at this moment.

"Hello!" he barked this time, taking a few cautious steps toward the kitchen.

Gina didn't even flinch when Mr. Grin came out from behind the wall. Hopefully, she didn't even remember who it was.

Mr. Grin threw up his hands.

"Wait! Wait!" he said.

Now Jack was confused. That didn't sound at all like Mr. Grin.

"Sam?" he said.

"The new body's pretty much like the old body, don't you think?"

It still looked like John Briggs to Jack but he guessed, with some scruff around the face and some longer hair, some time, he would actually look a little bit like Sam.

"I had a fucked up trip you wouldn't believe," Sam said. "I dreamed I was dead and then my soul left its body because it was all mangled and maybe even dead and then I found this one and then when I woke up, I looked like this. But I couldn't even remember what I used to look like. Fucked up shit. Hey, babes," he said to Gina, coming over and giving her a kiss on the cheek.

Jack couldn't help the small tremor that ran up his spine.

Sam grinned at Jack and told him he was glad everything worked out okay.

Jack patted him on the arm and said, "I don't think you should ever smile around me again."

About the Author

Andersen Prunty lives in Ohio.
Visit him online at notandersenprunty.com.

Other Grindhouse Press Titles

Samantha Kolesnik

#067__*Deathripping: Collected Horror Stories* by Andersen Prunty
#066__*Depraved* by Bryan Smith
#065__*Crazytimes* by Scott Cole
#064__*Blood Relations* by Kristopher Triana
#063__*The Perfectly Fine House* by Stephen Kozeniewski
and Wile E. Young
#062__*Savage Mountain* by John Quick
#061__*Cocksucker* by Lucas Milliron
#060__*Luciferin* by J. Peter W.
#059__*The Fucking Zombie Apocalypse* by Bryan Smith
#058__*True Crime* by Samantha Kolesnik
#057__*The Cycle* by John Wayne Comunale
#056__*A Voice So Soft* by Patrick Lacey
#055__*Merciless* by Bryan Smith
#054__*The Long Shadows of October* by Kristopher Triana
#053__*House of Blood* by Bryan Smith
#052__*The Freakshow* by Bryan Smith
#051__*Dirty Rotten Hippies and Other Stories* by Bryan Smith
#050__*Rites of Extinction* by Matt Serafini
#049__*Saint Sadist* by Lucas Mangum
#048__*Neon Dies At Dawn* by Andersen Prunty
#047__*Halloween Fiend* by C.V. Hunt
#046__*Limbs: A Love Story* by Tim Meyer
#045__*As Seen On T.V.* by John Wayne Comunale
#044__*Where Stars Won't Shine* by Patrick Lacey
#043__*Kinfolk* by Matt Kurtz
#042__*Kill For Satan!* by Bryan Smith
#041__*Dead Stripper Storage* by Bryan Smith
#040__*Triple Axe* by Scott Cole
#039__*Scummer* by John Wayne Comunale
#038__*Cockblock* by C.V. Hunt
#037__*Irrationalia* by Andersen Prunty
#036__*Full Brutal* by Kristopher Triana
#666__*Satanic Summer* by Andersen Prunty
#035__*Office Mutant* by Pete Risley
#034__*Death Pacts and Left-Hand Paths* by John Wayne Comunale
#033__*Home Is Where the Horror Is* by C.V. Hunt
#032__*This Town Needs A Monster* by Andersen Prunty
#031__*The Fetishists* by A.S. Coomer